THE BLACKHART BLADES

NP Novellas:

1. Universal Language – **Tim Major**
2. Worldshifter – **Paul Di Filippo**
3. May Day – **Emma Coleman**
4. Requiem for an Astronaut – **Daniel Bennett**
5. Rose Knot – **Kari Sperring**
6. On Arcturus VII – **Eric Brown**
7. Fish! – **Ida Keogh**
8. My Mother Murdered the Moon – **Stephen Deas**
9. Visions of Ruin – **Mark West**
10. Entropy of Loss – **Stewart Hotston**
11. Telling the Bees – **Emma K. Leadley**
12. The Blackhart Blades – **David Gullen**

THE BLACKHART BLADES

David Gullen

NewCon Press
England

First published in the UK July 2023 by
NewCon Press
41 Wheatsheaf Road,
Alconbury Weston,
Cambs, PE28 4LF

NPN021 (limited edition hardback)
NPN023 (paperback)

10 9 8 7 6 5 4 3 2 1

ISBN:

978-1-914953-52-1 (hardback)
978-1-914953-54-5 (paperback)

Cover layout and design by Ian Whates

Typesetting and editorial meddling by Ian Whates

One

'So, I might have found us a job,' Little Evelyn said when she came back from the castle town with food and firewood.

'A job?' Quicksilver limped over. He looked puzzled. 'I thought we were passing through.'

'We are. And we already have a job. A duty.' Irion frowned and pulled her furs up around her neck. Grud, it was cold. She caught Mace's eye as the big, slow, and surprisingly smart warrior significantly patted the purse at her hip and shook her head.

'We were,' Irion sighed. 'Well done, Evelyn, what's this job?'

Evelyn waved a piece of paper, torn at the four corners. 'It's a good 'un. Well, I'm pretty certain it is. It's a job, anyways.'

Irion, with steel grey eyes and a height more than most men, knew how to use her advantages in a fight. Oh, she could fight all right, and after a childhood of brawling and battling, she knew how to pick her battles too. She held out her hand for the piece of paper and read, then passed it to Mace, who did the same, shrugged, and passed it back. 'All right,' Irion said. 'We'll take a look.'

Irion, Mace, and Evelyn walked down into town, then up through the market under the walls of Steynhylda castle to the gatehouse. As they arrived, a meatily large woman with greasy, shining cheeks and arms like hams emerged dragging a wailing, protesting youth by his ear through the sally port.

She flung him forwards, stuck out a foot and the lad went sprawling in the muck. 'Steal from the king's kitchen would you? Back to the gutter you go.' She wiped her hands on her apron, a garment that appeared never to have been washed, turned Irion a look of incurious belligerence and stomped back into the castle.

Irion sighed, life was the same the world over. They'd detoured this way simply for some peace and quiet, an escape from the turmoil of the apparently unstoppable expansion of Veng the Usurper's empire. An expansion which threatened to suck every able-bodied woman and man into the insatiable maw of Veng's army. But detours cost money, especially ones as long and slow as this. Despite the need to work, Irion didn't mind. Zangomar was a small, peaceful mountain kingdom and by all accounts King Yogi was a lot better than most kings, which made him about a million times nicer than Veng.

The four castle guards were relaxed but alert, their steel and leather armour good quality and in good repair. Sword or mace, spear and shield, they were too well equipped and not pretty enough to be pure ornament. Irion approved of the way two of them blocked their path and two hung back. She also noticed that while the turret flags flew at the tops of their masts each guard wore a white arm band embroidered with the Eagle and Serpent of Zangomar.

'We're here about the job,' she said, and held up the copy of the proclamation Evelyn had brought back to their camp.

Wanted!

~

Men and Women of quality and experience,
unafraid of getting their hands dirty.

~~

"Those who would challenge fate,
Must know themselves 'fore time & tide,
Sweep all away 'pon that final, lonesome ride."

~~~

Reward commensurate with results!!

~~~~

Apply to: Sieur Bon Banacort, Steward to the King
The Castle, Steynhylda, Zangomar.

~~~~~

By Appointment.

~~~~~~

'We weren't sure if that meant we needed an appointment or –?'

One of the guards, stocky, with a weather-seamed face and steady blue eyes, worked his jaw. 'It means him, Banacort, he's appointed.'

Evelyn bobbed her head. 'Told you.'

'So we can just –?' Irion gestured towards the open sally-port in the great door.

The guard handed his spear to his companion. 'I'll walk you in.'

As they stepped through the little door into the tunnel Mace whispered in Irion's ear. 'Proper guards, gate's shut, and portcullis is half down.'

Irion glanced back and took it all in. 'I see it.'

The guard watched them patiently. 'If you don't mind me saying, you don't look like typical sell-swords.'

'We're not,' Irion said. 'But we do get things done.'

Banacort could not see them straight away, so the guard led them to the refectory where platters of cold cuts, red apples, onions, yellow cheese, fresh bread, smoked fish, and jugs of small beer awaited all-comers.

A group of eight dour men sat at one corner bench. Dark, fair, hulking or slight, each was silent, watching. They looked on not with an attitude suggesting they owned the place, but as if they planned to. Every single one of them sat with their back to the wall. Hunched over their food and drink, they wore a motley of shabby armour: studded leather, a piece of plate, a ragged coat of fence. Their weapons – a variety of short swords, maces, clubs, and ugly bill-hooks – hung at their hips or lay on the table.

Evelyn slipped an apple into her pocket and cut herself some bread and cheese. The men at the corner bench watched not with the attitude that they owned her, but that they planned to. She joined Irion and Mace at a bench in the opposite corner, not too far from the door.

'You notice the look the guard gave that lot,' Mace said under her breath.

'Indeed.' Irion nodded towards the eight and raised a hand. The men looked back and ate with their knives and made no reply. Irion and Mace knew that look well. It waited for drink stronger than small beer and a night in a dark place where nobody cared about screams and cries for help.

'This place needs a fire,' Irion said.

'It needs a broom,' Mace muttered.

None of the eight men wore white arm bands.

After an uncomfortable half hour the guard escorted them to the chilly main hall, where Sieur Bon Banacort, upright, sturdy, and firm of jaw, but with eyes too close together and a chin too heavy to be truly handsome, greeted them with effusive warmth.

'Welcome, most welcome. Needs must, come the hour, come the... person,' he babbled. He clasped Irion's hands in both of his, shaking them like maracas and holding on far too long. 'Oh my, madam, your hands are frozen. In my room burns a friendly fire. There is also good brandy, and –' Banacort gave the still-lingering gatehouse guard a significant look, 'privacy.'

'A fire would be very welcome.'

Banacort led the way on long-toed slippers, his robes of blue and silver swept the ground with each long stride.

'It's her name,' Mace told him as they walked. 'Irion the Cold. Cold hands, colder heart.'

'Indeed. And you are?'

Mace noticed he had a bald patch. Nothing wrong with that, it was the condition of men, but he'd tried to conceal it with an over-comb. She gave him her best fight-stopping look. 'Mace.'

'Of course it is. Well, here we are.' Banacort leaned against a heavy oak door, the wood grey with age, and heaved it open. Beyond it, his rooms were spacious and uncluttered. A table of eight legs, wide and deep, stood across the middle of the room, set with a scatter of candelabra and paperweights. An ink-pot, paper and quills stood at one end. Light fell from three high, narrow windows; shelves stacked with books and scrolls lined one wall. A merry fire burned in the open hearth, flanked by cushioned benches. All was scrupulously clean and dust-free. Irion went to the fire and warmed her hands. Banacort set out four crystal cups on the table and poured brandy from a silver decanter.

Little Evelyn knocked hers back in one and bared her teeth. 'Nice. So, what's the job?'

Banacort refilled her cup. 'I can't quite place your accent, madam.'

'Few people can, and to answer your next question, I wish I knew.'

'Ah, home.' Banacort smiled up at the rafters and intoned:

'That fond place for'er beyond our grasp,

Yet lodged, as 'twere, by arrow's barb,

Deep within the heart.'

Evelyn looked like she'd just swallowed a fly. 'So, yeah, right. Like I said, what's the job?'

'Yes, decisive and to the point!' Banacort cut the air with the edge of his palm. 'I like it.' He turned to face the fire. 'Madam Irion, I take it you lead your troop?'

'I do not. We are the Blackhart Blades, and Dante Blackhart leads. I am his lieutenant.'

'Sir Blackhart is indisposed?'

'Sir Blackhart doesn't negotiate. I speak with his voice.'

'As do I for the kingdom of Zangomar.' Banacort's shoulders sagged. 'Except, and here's the first thing upon which I must have your uttermost oath of silence before we even begin –'

'Then you have it, from all of us,' Irion said before Mace could speak. 'Including those of us back at our camp.'

'Excellent. Good.' Banacort cleared his throat and tugged down his robe. Irion gestured for him to continue.

'So, then. Well, this is it, you see, the thing. In the kingdom there's a gap, a void, a lacuna.' Banacort laughed nervously.

'He who once bestrode the ramparts of our fate,

As some benign titan of aeons past,

Once kept great Chronos himself at bay,

And held him from the gate.

Where looketh now we for–?'

'Just say it,' Mace said.

Banacort gave an odd liquid shudder from head to toes, then drained his own brandy cup. He touched his own arm band. 'King Yogi is dead.'

'Oh-ho, one of those is it?' Evelyn raised her cup in toast. 'The king is dead, long live the king.'

'Not quite.'

'Do you write that stuff yourself?'

Banacort tipped his head from side to side. 'It's a work in progress.'

'I quite liked it.'

'Why, thank you, I'd be happy to read you more –'

'You said, "The first thing",' Mace said.

'Yes.' Now the news was out Banacort became professional and serious. 'A week ago King Yogi, who had been complaining of breathlessness and pain in his arms for some time, died in his sleep. This was common knowledge, and the kingdom still mourned his passing. What is less well known is that the King's daughter and sole heir, the former Princess and now *Queen* Zaphron, refuses to take on his duties.

'The very day after her father died, she rushed into her rooms at the top of the eastern tower, called the Peacock tower because it once housed a roost of those magnificent birds and about which there is a rather interesting –' Banacort's flow of words faltered under Mace's blank stare. 'Anyway, since then she has refused to show herself.'

'Struck low by grief, overwhelmed by duty?' Irion said.

'One can only speculate.' An odd smile flickered around Banacort's mouth that Irion put down to incipient hysteria held on a tight leash. 'She refuses to put in any kind of appearance. No word, not even a written note.'

'I have to ask this, but is she actually still alive?'

'I am certain. My men guard the tower day and night. No possible harm could have come to her.'

'In her grief could she have –?' Irion made a wrist-slitting gesture with her thumb.

'It's not in her nature. And at the risk of being crude,' he pinched his nose.

'Maybe she and I could have a chat,' Evelyn said. 'This place is full of men, she might just need a bit of girl talk.'

'A kind thought, but I'm afraid protocol only bends so far.'

'So she's effectively abdicated.' Irion turned back to the fire. 'Who's next in line?'

'And there you have it. There isn't anyone.'

'Nobody? No by-blows, no extended family, no pretenders?'

'Not that we can find. Yogi, long may he rest in peace, was the only child of an only child, and so was his late wife. And her family was not, shall we say, ennobled.'

'Married for love. Sensible man,' Mace said.

'Perhaps.' Banacort moved quills, paper, wax and seals around on the table. 'There's something else. Some years ago, Princess Zaphron went on the traditional grand tour, a rite of passage, coming of age thing, visiting the great sites of antiquity, the cities and palaces of the neighbouring kingdoms.' Banacort looked up from the table. 'This was before Veng, you understand.'

'While there actually were neighbouring kingdoms and royal palaces,' Mace said.

'Quite.' Banacort moved all the objects into a neat line. 'She brought someone back with her, a man called Black Talahan. By the time she had returned to Zangomar they had been together long enough for him to have become her confidante, a favourite.'

'Ooh, love, was it?' Evelyn said.

'Not at all. He is older than Yogi was himself.'

Irion stood, her back to the fire. 'And that was a problem how?'

'It wasn't, at the time. Talahan was well liked and got on with the King. In fact Yogi made him general of the army, such as it is. A sinecure really, but Talahan smartened things up.'

'So what's the actual problem here?'

'The night young Queen Zaphron disappeared the treasury was emptied. Since then, Talahan has been locked up in Hardknot Keep and won't talk to anyone.'

This was getting complicated. 'So, you want us to persuade Queen Zaphron out of her rooms, evading all your niceties of protocol, using methods you can effectively deny, and –'

'No, I want you to kill Talahan and restore the treasure to the treasury. Then you'll get paid, handsomely, and I can pay for the running of the kingdom before it collapses into anarchy. Once that is done, yes, please, by all means persuade Queen Zaphron to come out. And I do mean by all means.'

Mace spoke slowly and definitely. 'We get the job done, but we don't do "by all means".'

Banacort waved her comment away. 'As your conscience dictates.'

Irion ordered her thoughts on the situation. The kingdom of Zangomar was effectively an enormous mountains-encircled valley. While there were passes through those mountains, they were cold, high, difficult places. The valley mouth was effectively the only way caravans, wheeled transport, and anything approaching an army, could enter. Hardknot Keep guarded a pinch-point near the valley mouth, where the mountains drew together and the river Skrune cut down deep on one side in a series of wild rapids. A small plateau, less than a good bowshot across, separated the gorge from the keep. While the keep itself was solid, the double curtain walls crossing the plateau had been allowed to fall into disrepair. It was the way they had come themselves, scrambling over the fallen masonry, intending to make for one of those high passes on foot, buy horses on the far side and travel onwards to avoid Veng.

Irion thoughtfully sipped her brandy. 'How many men does Talahan have?'

'Perhaps one hundred and fifty.'

This seemed eminently doable, especially if they had a bit of help. 'Who are those men in the refectory?'

'Some of my personal escort. And before you ask, they stay here, in the castle with me. The King is dead, the Queen is *incommunicado*; I am, so to speak, the last pole in the tent. I can take no chances.'

'You suspect –?'

Banacort puffed his cheeks. 'The wind, nothing, everything.'

'Veng?'

'Veng has a more direct way.'

'That she does.'

Everyone thought about Veng's massed forces and how she worked. Personal attention came after conquest, not before. Usually seated on the end of a twenty-foot sharpened pole.

'Then how many men in your army?'

Banacort gave a tight smile. 'About one hundred and fifty.'

Grud's sake. 'All right. Anything else?'

'Well, I don't believe it myself, but some say there's a ghost.'

'Cold hands, colder heart, that was very good,' Irion said as they walked back through the town.

Mace smiled. 'I thought I might use it again.'

'That Banacort's a proper gobshite.' Irion and Mace gave Evelyn a puzzled look. 'Arse-conker, shit gibbon. And those men of his...'

'You don't like him,' Irion said.

'Like's got nothing to do with it. I'm just sayin', he's not a geezer.'

'I agree, or at least I think I do,' Mace said. 'A man of contradictions, vain and pompous, a show-off, insecure, yet competent and clever. Dangerous.'

'Like I said, a right palace weasel.'

'I'll give you that,' Mace said. 'I think he likes being in charge. And those men of his are spelled "Trouble".'

The blond-haired lad they had seen being slung out of the castle sat on a broken millstone just outside the town wall. Irion noted how he'd washed his hands and face and otherwise cleaned himself up as best he could. He also didn't have his hand out, another point in his favour.

He stepped up smartly as they passed by. 'If you please, madam, I would like to join your troupe.'

Well-spoken, well-made, and not entirely lacking in boldness. Even so. 'Why are you talking to my feet, lad?'

He straightened and met her eye. Good. 'Please, madam. I'll work for food, that's all I ask.'

'What can you do?'

'I can cook.'

'We have a cook. A fine, fine cook.' Irion held out three copper pennies. 'Good luck.'

'I could work for him!'

'Brian the Knifewife works alone.'

'Brian the–! But... he's the greatest living...' the boy spluttered, but still did not take the money. Irion gestured that he should and again he waved it away. 'That'll feed me for two days. I'd rather have nothing and a...' His words tailed off and he looked bitterly towards the castle.

'Home?' Evelyn said softly.

His lips were pressed together. Hard. He blinked and brushed away an angry tear. 'I'm not a thief.'

'Never said you were,' Irion said. 'And we still have a cook.'

Mace held up a finger. 'How long did you work in the castle kitchens?'

'All my life. At least, as long as I can remember.'

'So you know the castle well?'

'Like the back of my hand.'

'That's useful.'

Irion simply nodded and started walking. Evelyn followed on.

'What's your name, lad?' Mace said.

'Bobbins. I was a foundling, the seamstress who took me in called me her little bobbins, except I'm not so little now, so...'

'I'm Mace,' Mace said. 'I started out with another name but I didn't like it. I chose this one myself.'

'Bobbins does for me.'

'Come on, let's catch them up.' Mace set off with a long-legged, ground-eating stride. Bobbins hesitated, then started after her. At first he tried to match her step for step, gave up and settled into his own easy lope.

'Thank you, I'll work hard, I'm a good worker.'

'I'm sure.'

'I'm not a thief.'

'I reckoned that. What's the story?'

'It was the ghost.'

Mace walked in silence until they caught up with Irion and Evelyn. 'This is Little Evelyn, and this – this is Irion the Cold.'

Mace dropped her voice an octave, 'Cold hands, and a colder heart.'

'It's a curse,' Irion waved Mace's words away. 'I've been cursed to never to have warm hands or feet. Heart's fine.'

'And this is Bobbins. He has a story about a famished ghost.'

They'd made camp west of the last village before Hardknot Keep, a settlement large enough to have its own smithy. Flanked on both sides by stands of mountain ash and birch, an ice-cold stream dropped straight down a high cliff into a deep pool before babbling away to join the Skrune, half a mile distant. On one side the cliff beetled out into a deep overhang, sheltered and airy, it was a good place for both sleeping and a fire.

Irion whistled her signal and Quicksilver emerged from cover. He wore a green felt cap folded into a hunter's peak; a dark red cloak slung over one shoulder revealed a green linen shirt and a knee-length woollen kilt patched in various blues and greens. He held a powerful composite bow, and a quiver hung at his hip. His legs were bare, though he wore a sturdy ankle boot on his right foot.

Bobbins tried not to stare at his left leg: a supple, jointed thing apparently made of brass and bronze to just above the knee. It was chased all over with intricate curlicues and knotwork that, if it had been a leg of flesh and bone, would have emphasised the muscles and sinews.

'Quicksilver, meet Bobbins,' Irion said. 'He'll be staying with us a while.'

'Lad.'

'Sir.'

'Not a "Sir", oh no, never that.' Quicksilver's voice was a soft rasp, as was his laugh. 'What can you do?'

'I can cook.'

Quicksilver looked behind him to where a bull-chested man with a square head and close-cropped black beard and hair worked beside the fire. A flat stone slab had been set across three rocks to form a rough table, currently piled with a variety of vegetables.

As Bobbins watched, the man's hands blurred, far faster than the eye could follow, and the mixed leaves, roots, stems and pods resolved into separate heaps, each chopped, sliced, or diced as required.

'We have a cook,' Quicksilver said.

Brian the Knifewife looked up from the table, cleaned his knife, stropped it on the leather hanging at his waist and sheathed it in one of the bandoliers criss-crossing his chest.

'This is Bobbins,' Evelyn said as he came over. 'And he's got a story about a hungry goat.'

The ghost first appeared soon after the King died, though Bobbins said it took a while for the castle inhabitants to put two and two together.

'At first everyone thought it was just the wind, a dreary moaning that moved around the castle.'

Then it started taking food.

'And that's where you come in?' Irion said.

'Yes.' Bobbins sat with clenched fists. 'And out.'

'I was the only one saw it,' Bobbins said. 'Because I was the only one working that late in the kitchens, washing pots and scouring pans. I never had my own room, so I slept down there too. The Kitchen's lovely and warm all year round. That morning you first came in, I heard that moaning sound and saw food rise up into the air and disappear in front of my eyes. It was quality stuff for the upper rooms, except–'

'Except nobody believed you.'

Bobbins reflexively rubbed his ear. Evelyn reached out a sympathetic hand. 'Always blame the weak, the ones with no one else to blame. It's the same all the world, the *worlds* over.'

'They thought I'd stolen it, eaten it and then made up a story.'

Now Quicksilver was intrigued. 'What time of day was this?'

'Early morning, soon after sunrise.'

Irion caught the direction of Quicksilver's question. 'Not a noctambulo, then. And it's not hiding anything so neither is it a droll. Nevertheless, a spirit unable to pass beyond hearth and home.'

Mace nodded thoughtfully. 'King Yogi died peacefully of old age, a life well lived. There would seem to be no reason for him not to pass on to the white shores.'

'A domovoy then?' Quicksilver said. 'It explains the sounds.'

'It would seem so. Poor girl.'

'Which girl?' Then realisation dawned, wide-eyed, Bobbins covered his mouth with his hand. 'Oh no.'

'So, we kill this one man and this Sieur Bon Banacort gives us one quarter of the kingdom's entire treasury?' Quicksilver said.

'That's about it.' Irion shuffled closer to the fire. Then, to Bobbins great relief, she said, 'Except we don't kill, we extract, softly-softly, and then we have a quiet word.'

'And Banacort agreed to it, just like that?'

'We haggled a bit, but now you mention it.' Mace could have kicked herself. If it was a deal that sounded too good to be true, then it most likely was. Banacort had played to their straightened circumstances, and the unthinking greed that lay somewhere inside every woman and man.

'You trust him?'

'I don't trust anyone,' Irion scowled. 'Well, I trust you, and Evelyn, and Mace, and Brian, and Dante Blackhart.'

Quicksilver's soft laugh rasped. 'Blackhart's easy to trust.'

'Why's that?' Bobbins said, disappointed that he wasn't on the list.

Mace reached over and ruffled his hair. 'Because he's dead. That's what brought us here in the first place, we're taking him home.'

Bobbins looked around nervously but could see nothing approaching the size of a coffin or corpse.

'Just his heart.' Irion hefted a richly lacquered dark rosewood chest, secured with two padlocked black iron bands.

'What do you know of the keep, lad?' Quicksilver said.

Bobbins had been there several times over the years and he described what he knew as best as he remembered. A high curtain wall with towers at each corner sheltered stables, forge, cookhouse and quarters. A massive central redoubt, accessible only by a high and narrow external stair, held stores and a well sunk beneath an open hall. Two more floors lay above.

It was good information and Irion was pleased. She repeated it back to Bobbins and he agreed her understanding was correct.

'Tonight?' Mace said.

'Tonight.'

'Method?'

'Over the wall, up to the roof and down from the top.' Irion considered Bobbins, listening attentively and understanding little. 'Do you mind heights, lad?'

Bobbins had never had much cause to think about it, but did so now. 'Yes, probably.'

'You'll get used to it.'

Pots rattled, banged and scraped over by Brian's stone table followed by the sound of a knife dicing garnish so fast it sounded like sheets tearing. Then Brian approached, carrying six wooden platters laden with food, two in his left hand, two balanced on his forearm, and two more in his right. He more or less threw down five of the plates and by some miracle each landed in a lap with the food elegantly arranged, along with cutlery in a linen wrap.

'And what do we have tonight?' Quicksilver said.

'Clobbers, steeped in argent belhumes,' Brian said, then hunched over his plate and tucked in.

Bobbins looked down at the meal. It smelled delicious, and looked entirely like peppered venison steak, with potatoes braised in butter and mushrooms simmered in a red wine and onion sauce. There was even mustard. It occurred to him that he was utterly ravenous.

They ate in a hungry, companionable silence. From somewhere a bowl of fresh-baked bread rolls had appeared. Bobbins waited, then took the last roll to mop up the mix of savoury juices, wine, and butter. A wine skin was passed around and Bobbins took a mouthful of red wine rich with berry flavours. Perched on a flat rock, under a darkening twilight sky beside a smouldering fire in the company of near-strangers, he was convinced it was the finest meal he had ever eaten. He looked at Brian in awe. 'That was amazing.'

Brian pressed his hands together as if in prayer, and bowed, then gathered up the empty plates.

'I can clean them, and the pans too,' Bobbins begged. 'Please let me.'

Brian frowned, then nodded and handed over the platters and cutlery. Bobbins took them to the pool and scoured them with handfuls of fine grit lodged among the rocks in the shallows, then did the same with the pans and pots. He scoured them until every speck of food and fire mark was gone and his hands shone pink and raw from the icy water and rough sand.

When he was done he carried them back to Brian's table. Brian met him halfway and took everything without comment. Bobbins returned to the fire.

'How does he cook like that? Come to that, where does he find mushrooms and venison around here?'

'It's his gift,' Mace said.

'Gifts and curses.' Despite his solid bulk Brian's voice was high and softly sweet. 'When you think about it, they're much the same thing.'

Irion idly swung a three-pronged iron grapnel from the end of a stout rope.

'Isn't that a bit heavy to throw so high?' Bobbins said.

'It's a magic rope and weighs next to nothing.'

Bobbins took up the coils and was surprised to find they weighed no more than a goose-down pillow.

'What's more, knots never come undone until I say "Rope, to me."' Irion suppressed a hiss of pain as the knot in the grapnel's eye flowed apart and it dropped onto her foot. 'Like that.'

'Can I have a try?'

'No. Get some rest, we're off at midnight.'

Bobbins lay beside the fire under a borrowed blanket, his head pillowed on his hands. Yesterday he had been a pot-boy; in a few hours he would be taking part in a night-time assault on Hardknot Keep to kidnap the general of the army. He felt too excited, and too anxious, to sleep. He had never fought with weapons, he had never, unless you counted scrumping autumn apples from a farm orchard, broken any law.

We're not breaking law now, he told himself. *We're working for the King's Steward.*

Seemingly moments later he woke to Evelyn kicking his foot. 'Wake up, Bobbins, time to earn your keep.' She laughed at her own joke, '"Keep", get it?'

Bobbins hastily made himself ready. A mouthful of water, a swift look around the camp. The fire was down to embers, stars glittered in a clear sky. Everyone else was up and ready. Mace carried the biggest sword Bobbins had ever seen sheathed in a back-scabbard, Irion wore the rope coiled over her shoulder, Quicksilver had strung his bow, a full quiver hung at his hip. He looked for Evelyn, but she was nowhere to be seen. He went to Irion. 'What do I do?'

'Stay in camp and keep watch with Brian.'

Bobbins took in the news with a mixture of disappointment and relief. 'I thought –'

'You thought wrong.' Tension compressed Irion's lips into a thin line. 'You stay in camp.' A smile tugged the corner of her mouth and was gone. 'This time.'

Three hours' careful walking through the dark took them around the nameless village and down into the shadowed gloom under the walls of the keep.

Irion carefully spooled the rope in open coils on the ground, turning it as she went so that it lay flat and free of kinks. Then she settled her stance and wound the grapnel, faster and faster, her eye fixed on the high battlements.

Quicksilver's hand came down on Evelyn's shoulder. 'Give her some space.'

Evelyn stepped back, blended into the shadows, and was *gone*. It was a knack Quicksilver deeply envied.

Irion let fly; the grapnel soared up into the air pulling the rope behind.

'That's a tad high,' Quicksilver said under his breath.

Still gaining height, the grapnel soared over the battlements and arced down into the keep. Quicksilver clumped forwards and put his booted foot on the end of the rapidly uncoiling rope.

Deep in the keep came a clang, a startled yelp, then the sounds of a man-at-arms in half-plate with spear and shield tumbling down a flight of stone steps.

Irion, Quicksilver, Evelyn, and Mace winced with every crash and clatter.

'Ah,' Mace said. 'Um.'

Nobody else said a word.

Deep inside the keep a trumpet blew alarum, and then, another. High in the redoubt a light flickered, steadied, and shone bright.

'We should probably –' Mace jerked her thumb over her shoulder towards the way they had come.

'Rope, to me,' Irion said a little sadly.

Come sunrise, Bobbins walked to the nearby village to buy another grapnel. It was a small place, the home for a dozen families of goatherds and high valley farmers, but it was large enough to have its own inn, The First and Last, a diminutive all-comers temple, and a forge. It was there that he found Quiet Arthur, the blacksmith. Arthur had a good collection of second-hand three, four, and even five-prong grapnels.

He would have bought two but the smith's prices were steep and so he chose a three-pronged one almost identical to that Irion once had.

'It's a seller's market, the keep let me have them for next to nothing,' Arthur explained as he worked on beating a deep dent out of a conical helmet.

'Oh?' Bobbins shouted over the sound of Arthur's work, with the wide-eyed innocence of a stranger passing through. 'There's a keep?'

Arthur tipped his chin towards the high pass. 'Last night, was that you?'

'No,' Bobbins declared with utter conviction, sweating now from the heat of the forge. 'That wasn't me what?'

Arthur grinned and shook his head.

Bobbins picked up the grapnel and made to go.

'Those walls aren't as high as they look,' Arthur said.

'Oh?'

Quiet Arthur tapped his nose. 'That Black Talahan's a wizard.'

'The walls of the keep are enchanted to look higher than they are,' Bobbins said on his return to the Blades camp.

Evelyn rolled her eyes. 'And just how do you know that?'

'The blacksmith told me.'

'Is he a mage, then? Are you a mage?'

'No, but he said Talahan was, and he also has more second-hand grapnels than you can wag a rope at. The keep lets him have them wholesale.'

Irion massaged her temple. 'Grud's sake.'

Irion, Mace, and Evelyn went back to the castle. Bon Banacort granted them an immediate audience.

'Why didn't you tell us Talahan was a wizard?' Irion demanded.

'Because he's not, not a real one. Do you think I'd knowingly send you all to your deaths against a true magus of the eleven-fold way?'

They sat with Banacort around his campaign table, sipping mild black ale and nibbling on sweet crackers and hard yellow cheese.

'Seventeenth would be worse, to be honest,' Mace said.

The silence drew out until it was uncomfortable.

'Look, he knows a few bits and pieces. Ever since he's been here he's been in correspondence with one of the lesser Luminaries of Kelophase. He sends them gold, they send him a scroll with a cantrip or two. As I understand it that's where most of his pay went.'

'So, he is a magus,' Irion said.

'Untutored, and incomplete at the most basic levels. I admit he has some innate talent otherwise the Luminaries would not have indulged him with correspondence, but he's not had the tutoring or the years, nay, decades, of study, to become a...'

'An unstoppable death-machine?' Evelyn suggested.

'That's not quite how I would put it.'

'How would you put it? Exactly?'

Another silence stretched away, angrier and more uncompromising than before. Banacort took a breath and began:

In times past, most ancient days,
When lords of might strove, one 'gainst t'other,
Legend and lore in fitful strife. Yeah, fire and ice,
Man beset by monster, husband by –'

Banacort tailed off under Mace's unremitting glare as she thought about all the terrible things she might do to his family.

'I thought perhaps some deeper context?' Banacort said.

Mace drew abstract patterns in the beer rings on the table. 'Look, it's not you, it's me.'

'Each to his –' Banacort made a gracious gesture, '–or her own. When I said Black Talahan's not a magus, believe me. He's a dabbler, a dilettante, a parvenu. I know for a fact he's only got to "L".'

'What?'

'The Luminaries of Kelophase are nothing if not pedantic. Teaching of the first fold begins with *Arbuthnot's Affable Appendage,* and proceeds alphabetically to *Ziliphant's Zoological Yammering*. Once these are mastered, study of fold the second commences with *Berthold's Over-friendly Fingers*, then–'

Irion leaned forwards. 'And you know this how?'

'I am Sieur Bon Banacort, Steward to the King-House of Yogi III, it is my job to know things. When I say Talahan has reached "L", then "L" it is. Most probably *Lakshmi's Happy Harvest*.' Banacort smiled queasily. 'Her *Winnowing* spell represents a bit of a step-change.'

Irion conceded the point. For all his pomp and pretention, Banacort was more than competent.

'How many attempts have been made on the keep?' Mace said.

'A few.' Banacort sat pinned by Irion's steady gaze. 'Several.'

'What happened to them?'

'They all departed. Alive and intact, I should add.' Banacort's gaze drifted towards the door. 'Is that what you now intend?'

'No,' Irion said. 'We like the deal, and our chances. We still have a few arrows in our quiver.'

'Well, that's good to know,' Quicksilver said when Irion and Mace returned to camp with the news.

'That they survived their attempts, or that they failed?' Mace said.

Irion seldom theorised, but when she did, she often hit the nail on the head. 'Banacort's usurped the throne. The kingdom of Zangomar has its own home-grown little Veng, but why? And more particularly, why now?'

'So Sieur Bonbon wossname is a cheese-head of the first water and is almost certainly going to back out of the deal,' Evelyn said. 'But he doesn't strike me as a Queen killer. Black Talahan on the other hand, I mean, the clue's in the name, innit?'

'Do you think?' Quicksilver snapped. 'Maybe he used to be a chimney sweep or a miner, or travelled in creosote. I mean, nobody calls me Hopalong and nobody thinks you're evil and calls you "Black Evelyn", do they?'

Evelyn looked down at her own forearm. 'Not like that, not any more,' she said quietly. 'I always thought I was more dark brown.' She looked up into Quicksilver's angry yet sympathetic eyes and shrugged. 'Anyways, I still say its him. Why else would he be sitting on the treasury, in a keep, and with half the army, and refusing to come out?'

'Almost the entire army,' Mace said. 'Perhaps because the princess, now the queen, asked him to?'

'Why would she do that?'

'To keep it safe from sticky fingers.'

'Ah,' Evelyn said, then slapped her thigh. 'Oh-ho. So what happened to the princess, and why did Banacort tell us she was missing?'

Mace turned to Irion. 'Why don't we just knock on Talahan's door and ask him?'

'Good idea, I like it.' Irion stood from where she was sitting beside fire and knocked the wood ash from her trousers. 'We have a plan. You, me, and Quicksilver.'

'Now?'

'No time like the present.'

Bobbins sat with Evelyn and watched her sharpen one of her bearded axes on a whetstone with long, even strokes. Over by the stone table Brian the Knifewife stropped his own blades.

'Where are you actually from, Evelyn?' Bobbins caught her narrow look and added, 'If you don't mind me asking.'

'I don't mind.' Evelyn slowed the pace of her honing. 'Down south aways.'

Bobbins frowned, puzzled, unsure about what to say next. 'Um, we *are* south.'

'North, then.'

Bobbins' mouth twisted. 'Why don't you trust me?'

The little camp fell silent as Evelyn stopped honing her blade. Over by the table Brian listened intently. He took a step forwards, then another.

Evelyn answered as gently as she could, not wanting to hurt more than was unavoidable. 'Because you're not one of us.' She softly punched his shoulder with her fist. 'Not yet.'

'Evelyn,' Brian admonished, 'time was when none of us were "one of us". For all his faults, all of his many, many faults, Dante Blackhart took us under his admittedly broken wing and helped each of us become who we wanted to be.'

'But you're Brian the Knifewife,' Bobbin said, still awed to be in the presence of such a legendary chef. 'How could you not be who you wanted to be?'

'Very easily, lad.' Brian settled next to him. 'I've cooked everything you can imagine, a few things you cannot, and once an entire meal from ingredients that did not exist.' Brian's eyes grew misty with the memory, 'A thousand different recipes for a score of kings and princes and queens. I tell you, people like that always think they know best, every single one of them.. "A little less Malmsey, Brian,", "A little more garlic". Half the time they wanted things out of season as if flavour and freshness and texture count for nothing. And more than once, if you can believe it, "Not enough gold."'

Bobbins stared. "You can eat gold?"

'You can shit it out later too,' Evelyn said.

Brian held up a finger. 'I just wanted to cook, lad. Cook food. Good food. Food that tastes like it came out of the ground or from the sea, or off the land. I wanted to use my own recipes and call them anything I liked, and have no one tell me too much this, Brian, not enough that, Brian. I –' Brian's voice had grown hard, he shook his head. 'I just wanted to cook.'

'And I'd like to learn,' Bobbins burst out. 'Given the chance.'

'Tell him, Evelyn,' Brian said. 'I say he's earned it.'

Evelyn took her axe and gave it a few more slow strokes on the stone. 'I don't know where I'm from, Bobbins. Or rather, I do, but I don't know how to get back there. There was a door, I shouldn't have gone through it, but I did, and it closed behind me. I walked through a shadow-land and now I'm here.'

'I'm sorry,' Bobbins said.

'Ah, it's all right,' Evelyn sighed. 'Life's different, but it's not so bad, though I do miss good coffee and cheap chocolate.'

Brian shook his head. 'I don't know what they are either. I tell you what, Bobbins, if you really want to learn to cook then I'll teach you, but first –'

'You will?' Bobbins jumped to his feet, 'You will?'

Brian held up a finger. 'But first, get yourself some decent knives.'

On the final approach to the keep Mace pulled a dagger from her boot, ready to hammer on the door with the pommel. It proved unnecessary as, with a bang and shudder and the sounds of metal sliding on metal then metal across wood, one of the heavy, time-weathered doors creaked open.

Mace held onto her dagger until she saw a single man awaited them, then sheathed it without fuss and walked forwards with Irion and Quicksilver.

He was still broad across the shoulders, and his back straight, but time and life had worked their mischief. One eye drooped a little and he favoured his right leg even when simply standing. His once-red beard was now mostly white. He wore long brown boots, armour on shins, chest, and forearms, and he dangled a three-pronged grapnel from his hand.

'Do you want this back?' Black Talahan said.

Irion burst out laughing and strode forward. 'Yes, please.'

'Neat trick with the rope,' Talahan said. 'I wouldn't mind a rope like that.'

'We can talk about that later.' Irion made the introductions.

'I was sorry to hear about Blackhart,' Talahan said. 'I met him once, long ago. We were on some road from here to there. He seemed troubled.'

'He was a troubled man.' Irion wanted to say more, that he was good and decent and trustworthy, that he was a friend. None of those words applied. 'He was all right, in his own way. For some reason I liked him.'

'So did I, though I still wonder why.'

That was Dante Blackhart all right.

Talahan was an amiable host and also let them see what they wanted to see. The keep was well provisioned, the men and women of the guard disciplined, alert, and well equipped. From the hall on the keep's second floor they watched the work being done to repair and reinforce the outer curtain wall that ran flat across the ground from the keep to the gorge, where the Skrune roared and seethed.

'It probably won't be finished in time,' Talahan said. 'No matter.'

Mace couldn't resist the bait. 'In time for what?'

'For Veng's army.'

Talahan fed them well, if simply, clearly buying in fresh produce from the mountain settlements beyond the keep in preference to using stores. The beer was cool, crisp, and very good. The grapnel sat pointedly at one end of the rough table and Irion found it hard to take her eyes off it.

'Um, sorry about your man. Is he all right?'

'He's fine. That's the thing about falling downstairs in armour – you're wearing armour.'

Talahan was particularly interested in Quicksilver's metal leg.

'I've never seen such fine work. It's fey isn't it?'

Quicksilver smiled to himself and sipped his ale. 'No, not the good folk.' At times like these Quicksilver was deliberately evasive. Irion and Mace let him have his moment. 'It was the Mer.'

'The Merfolk!' Talahan sat forwards. 'I'd heard, but never seen. Amazing.'

'I helped them once, and when I took a wound they helped me. Nevertheless, I had intruded and there was a price.'

'I would like to hear that tale.'

'A story for another day. For now, I shall say the price is always the price, and I like to think I now have a good leg, and a better one.'

'Indeed.' For a moment Talahan became introspective, then picked up the beer kettle. 'More ale?'

'A little,' Irion said.

Talahan was a good host, and remarkably well travelled. An hour slipped by, then another. The conversation ranged back and forth as they exchanged news and favourite anecdotes.

Irion leaned back in her chair. Her eyes roved the room, rested briefly on a stout, heavily padlocked door, and moved on. 'What can less than two hundred men and women do against Veng?'

'You think it's about buying time or setting an example?' Talahan tipped his head and smiled. 'You should go out there and talk to them. Really. This is their home, their lives. Yogi was a good king, a good *man*, and Queen Zaphron deserved a better chance than this. If they had been born to rule a mightier land perhaps the world could have been a different place.' Talahan laughed quietly at his own rhetoric. 'Perhaps.'

Mace sipped her ale thoughtfully. Black Talahan. These weren't the words of someone with a dark reputation. 'And Bon Banacort?'

'Whatever he's told you, it's probably not true.'

'This we had already guessed.'

At some point the ale stopped flowing and the platters of meat and bread lay empty.

Talahan pushed back his chair. 'I expect you'll want to be on your way.'

Mace opened her mouth to speak. Irion stilled her with a hand on her knee beneath the table. 'Thank you. It's been a pleasure to enjoy your company.'

'Likewise.' Talahan led them down through the narrow, enclosed stairway to the foot of the keep.

'Oh, one thing,' Irion stopped as they were half-way across the courtyard towards the open gate. 'Who killed Queen Zaphron?'

'Who told you she was dead?' Talahan said, then immediately realised his mistake.

And just like that everything changed.

The fingers of Talahan's off-hand moved in a quick, subtle gesture and two of the four men at the gate began to push it closed. Archers stood on the walls. Talahan took a step back, and then another, and the space between them was beyond sword cut or dagger thrust.

They would never make it to the gate. Irion made a gesture of her own and Quicksilver moved into position between her and Mace. The two women wrapped an arm around Quicksilver's waist and gripped his belt.

He bent his leg.

A net dropped over them.

Quicksilver jumped anyway, pulling the men holding the net fifteen feet into the air before they all tumbled down again.

Mace and Irion flung off the net, drew their swords and faced half a dozen circling men at arms. Both kept a hand on Quicksilver's sturdy belt. Quicksilver's bow was drawn, his arrow aimed steadily at Talahan's heart.

Talahan spoke seven syllables and made another simple gesture. The air between them shimmered into a glimmering V-shaped prow.

'Much as I'd like to see you jump again, are you sure you can make it over those high walls?'

'They're not as high as they look,' Mace growled.

'Ah, you worked that one out.'

'And that's Perdustin's Airy Prow, a spell of the third fold.'

Talahan acknowledged her insight. 'With regards to my magic Banacort believes what I let him believe.'

'Does he believe that's really a ghost?'

'I don't know.' Talahan drew his own blade and, despite his age, fell easily into a balanced fighter's stance. 'I expect he has his doubts.'

Solve one mystery and others replaced it. At times like these Mace's mind raced in so many directions her head swam. Talahan had as much as admitted that whatever had happened to Queen Zaphron was his doing, but why? Had she agreed? They knew and liked each other well, unless that was another of Banacort's lies, but if not did that mean they were working together now? And to what end?

The gate closed with a soft and heavy boom, Talahan's men formed into two groups of three: spear, sword, and shield, poised and filled with tension. Irion glanced up at the battlements, saw the archers stood with bows still only half-drawn and was grateful for their discipline. Hit or miss, a stray arrow would break this frozen moment and then– mayhem. If they had survived odds worse than this she was damned if she could remember when. Grud's sake, was this how it all ended?

Talahan relaxed out of his stance and sheathed his sword. 'I don't like killing, and I don't want to see any now. I'm also not sure if Perdustin's Prow will stop your arrow at this range. Frankly, I'd rather not find out. So now we've shown each other what we're capable of, shall we try this again?'

Although the gate was still closed, the archers on the walls and the men at arms in the courtyard stood down. Mace felt the tension leave Quicksilver's body as he relaxed the draw on his own bow. 'Banacort lied,' she said, then frowned. 'At least twice.'

Talahan's laughter blew through the courtyard. 'This is the great Sieur Bon Banacort we're talking about.' He gave an open-handed gesture towards the great gate. 'Leave, if you wish, but it must be beyond the wall and away. I cannot permit you to return to the castle.'

Straight towards Veng's army. Irion knew this situation was all her fault. She had been too clever by half with that last question and her timing was based on nothing but a desire to show off. 'This isn't our fight, we just want to be on our way to bury Blackhart. Will you accept my word?'

'At any other time.' Talahan sighed unhappily. 'I simply can't risk having Banacort at my back and knowing the truth.'

'About Queen Zaphron?'

'Amongst other things.'

'Your qualities as a mage.'

'That too.'

This was no choice at all. 'I have people at my camp.'

'Then I'll send some of mine to escort them here.'

'No need,' Quicksilver said. 'I'll go.'

Talahan became uncompromising. 'I must insist.'

'Quicksilver –' Irion held up a warning hand.

'You can't stop me,' said Quicksilver, who felt he had something to prove. And he was gone.

Quicksilver leaped far beyond bowshot in three enormous bounds, then ran the rest of the way to their camp. Evelyn, Brian, and Bobbins gathered around and he explained the situation.

Evelyn counted off on her fingers. 'So, our choices are these: One, abandon Mace and Irion and rat everything to Banacort. Not going to happen. Two, abandon Mace and Irion and leg it away over one of the high passes. Also not going to happen. Three, go to Talahan's keep and take our chances, which approximate zero or less, against Veng's army.'

Quicksilver sat with his better leg straight out, massaging the seamless join between the flesh and Merfolk metal. 'That seems about right.'

'All right,' Brian said after a while. 'All right, then.'

'Even from beyond the grave.' Evelyn started laughing, long and loud and humourless. 'Dante Blackhart makes his finest move.' She turned to Bobbins, 'Go back to the castle, lad, this has nothing to do with you.'

Cut by the bitterness in her words, only partly understanding, Bobbins stood where he was. 'Actually, I –'

'Bobbins is my apprentice, but in this case he's free to make up his own mind,' Brian said firmly. 'Everything changes here, lad, your entire life. All I'll say is that sometimes you live to regret the things you don't do more than the things you do. Go with your gut.'

Bobbins felt the pressure on his own heart lift. He would go with them, he *wanted* to go. Even if it meant... He began to gather the things they would need for the journey to the keep.

'I'll take that,' Quicksilver said as Bobbins moved towards Dante Blackhart's chest.

'Am I being a fool?' Bobbins asked Brian as they made their way towards the keep.

'Everyone's a fool, lad,' Brian said. They were in a steep part of the climb. After a few more steps he said, 'Welcome to the Blackhart Blades.'

'How's this,' Mace said. 'When the king died, Banacort decided to kill Zaphron and take the throne. You turned her invisible to save her life and absconded here with the treasury, so foiling Banacort's plans on two fronts. Now you can't risk going back to the castle to cancel the invisibility spell without risking both your lives and losing the keep and the gold.'

It made sense to Irion, Mace's plans and explanations usually did because they were usually right. That was why, to all intents and purposes, she let her decide most of the important matters. But Mace did not like to lead, that was Irion's job. And she did it well. She led the Blackhart Blades and given an army she could have led that too.

'What?' Talahan still glared at the place Quicksilver had stood, the air he had leapt through. Genuine anger flickered across his brow, then frustration and a weary kind of regret. 'Close enough, except the treasury gold was already here when I arrived, hidden in food sacks. I was as surprised as anyone. You have Banacort's wicked little design nailed down, but the strategy behind it eludes me. Yes, with one murder he has the kingdom, and I'm sure the loyal Bon Banacort, oath-sworn to the royal line as he is, can live with a single death on his conscience, even a queen's. But why now, with Veng's approach, what could he possibly gain?'

'With the royal lineage gone he sells the kingdom to save his own skin, and his position,' Mace said. 'Veng can't rule her empire alone, she needs viceroys to govern provinces. The treasury would have been his welcoming gift.'

'Yes, of course.' Talahan groped for a seat, found the edge of a horse trough and perched there. 'Put so bluntly it's obvious, I just don't share Banacort's talent for duplicity.'

'Oh, thanks a lot.'

'I'm sorry, I didn't mean that, it's just...'

'You're in a hole and everything you do keeps making it deeper.' Irion sat on the other end of the trough and gestured for him to continue.

'Banacort nearly got away with it,' Talahan said. 'We didn't exactly like each other, but I thought he was loyal and that was my mistake. I think, perhaps, he'd originally planned to persuade old Yogi, faced with the inevitability of Veng's army, to simply step aside. But Queen Zaphron is a different matter, so when her father died Banacort had little choice. Within hours of Yogi's death he'd set his men on Zaphron. A more wicked pack of cut-throats and child-stealers you'd never hope to see. They laid a trap but somehow she escaped and fled to her rooms in the Peacock tower. By sheer chance I was most of the way up the stairs myself, we'd previously arranged to talk about the defence of Zangomar. I heard the commotion – you'll be surprised how much noise four armed and armoured men in deadly pursuit can make – and saw Zaphron about to be run down.'

He's spinning this out, Irion realised. *There's something he's reluctant to get to.*

'Murderous, conscienceless thugs they might be, but like any sensible person Banacort's men are scared stiff of magic. I treated them to a quick show of some coloured lights and booming voices, which gave Zaphron enough time to push past me, and we raced on up.'

'And?'

'We had barely enough time for a brief conversation, and –'

'And you turned Zaphron invisible and made your own escape.'

'Not quite. I –' Talahan looked down at his boots, then up to Irion. 'I made a mistake.

'Cantrips of the first and second folds, needing only three and five syllables to invoke respectively, are easily memorised. Those of the third, needing seven, are less so, but any competent mageling can keep a handful in their mind until cast. The eleven syllables required to cast a spell from fold the fourth are another matter. Memorised straight from the holding scroll and then recited they are easy enough, but keeping those oblique and syntaxless phrases in the mind until needed is not easy. It is the point at which many aspiring wizardlings founder, never to again progress.

'Phandaal's Temporary Vanishing is a true spell from fold the fifth. I have cast it successfully before but had not read the scroll for three days. Somewhere in the thirteen syllables I made an error in pronunciation, or perhaps a syllable inversion or substitution.Most of the time this means the casting fails. 'That time it worked, or rather *something* worked and Zaphron disappeared. I don't need to be close to uncast a spell, I can release it like that,' he snapped his fingers. 'But I do need to know what it was I cast.'

'How do you know you made a mistake?'

'Two reasons. You feel these things in your bones at the final utterance, but by then you're committed. And Phandaal, being the unsurpassed brilliance that they were, ensured their "Vanishing" expired of its own accord when the sun next rose. Mine clearly didn't.'

'So you've invented a new spell, "Black Talahan's Permanent Whathaveyou", but you don't know what it exactly is, how to undo it, or how to cast it again,' Mace said.

Talahan looked rather downcast. 'Quite.'

'Or where you made the error?'

'It was somewhere in the third room. The final one.'

Now it was Irion and Mace's turn to be confused, and it was at this point they realised Quicksilver had returned with Evelyn, Brian, and Bobbins. By the mix of puzzled expressions on their faces it was clear they had been listening for some time.

'One way to visualise a spell is to think of it as a house,' Talahan said.

Irion frowned. 'That's not helping.'

'Perhaps I over simplify.'

'Works for me.' Brian shaped the air with his hands, 'I see all doors opening into all rooms at the same time.'

This only gave Irion a headache, but Talahan agreed enthusiastically. 'You have the talent?'

'I'm a cook,' Brian said. 'It's the same with a recipe, everything touches everything else. Why don't you experiment?'

'What do you suggest? Magical experimentation is an uncertain, dangerous business. Would you like to volunteer?'

'Use goats.'

'I could, but goats are not renowned for delivering accurate reports after the event.'

'It might narrow things down a bit.'

Talahan paced back and forth, massaging his temples. 'All this takes time and focus, and mental energy, none of which I have to spare at present.' He slumped back down on the corner of the trough. 'What does it matter anyway? At least Zaphron's safe.'

'If I might say, I think she'd rather be here,' Bobbins said.

Talahan gestured through the now open gate to the half-repaired walls. 'Do you think we can win here? Do you think I don't worry that self-serving cur Banacort might actually be doing the right thing?'

'He isn't,' Evelyn said with quiet determination.

'No, you're right, it's just that... I'm old, I'm tired, I'm filled with doubt.' Talahan sat with elbows on knees. 'Go, if you want. Just go' He waved them away like he was pushing at water. 'I shan't stop you.'

Mace saw Irion was about to say something and pulled her aside. 'We don't volunteer, remember? Blackhart's rule number one. You said it yourself, this isn't our fight.'

It wasn't a happy group that left, but leave they did. As it was late in the day Irion decided they would spend the night at the First and Last, the inn in the nearby village. Although small, it was clean and comfortable, and welcoming too.

There was only one room for sleeping, the hay loft above the stables. It was neither better nor worse than they were used to, though for Bobbins it felt like a kind of adventurous luxury.

'No candles, no lamps. If you burn my stables down I'll throw you into the fire.' The lantern-jawed innkeeper sounded like he meant it.

'Understood,' Irion said.

The taproom was as busy as it could be, with most of the village there and many others besides. The Blades squeezed themselves into a corner, knee pressed to knee around a small table.

Service was slow. The pot boy, tall and long in the face like his father, apologised. 'It's just me, me mam and dad. It's not always like this.'

The ale was so deliciously dark and rich you could almost chew it. Brian sat with fingers drumming on the table as they waited for their food to be served – dumplings swimming in a thick meat broth seasoned with rosemary, with hunks of that morning's bread and white goat's milk butter. Everyone watched over the rims of their mugs as he looked down at his bowl and doubtfully stirred the broth with his spoon. He bent low over the food, sniffed, tasted, grunted in approval, and began to eat.

When he had finished, Brian went out back. Soon the sounds of laughter erupted through the kitchen door, and not long after that the flow of food increased. Brian, beaming through his beard and with a towel over one arm, delivered two, three, and sometimes four bowls of food at once.

'He doesn't do this very often,' Irion said.

'I've never seen it,' Mace said.

All talk in tap room was of Veng, the keep, Queen Zaphron, and whether Black Talahan could be trusted.

'Excuse me, but I believe he can,' Irion said to the table of villagers next to them when that question of trust came up.

'That's all well and good,' Quiet Arthur, the blacksmith said, 'But can we trust you?'

Bobbins sipped his ale and spoke up. 'I'm from the castle, I've met Talahan and I think he's all right.'

Quiet Arthur leaned his hairy forearms on the table. 'So what do you think of that Sieur Bon Banacort?'

'I wouldn't like to say.'

The strong ale had gone to Little Evelyn's head. 'I would. He's an utter, utter c–'

Laughing a little too loud, Quicksilver clapped his hand over Evelyn's mouth. Rather than objecting, she leaned into his shoulder.

'I say he's all right,' one of the other villagers chipped in. 'He gave me a silver penny at the King's funeral.'

A general murmur of agreement swelled around the table.

Bobbins couldn't stop himself. 'Is that how you earn trust, with money?'

'Lad's got a point,' Arthur said and tapped his nose. 'Made a good point there.'

Bobbins took a breath. 'Arthur, do you make knives? Good ones, for the kitchen.'

'If I can get the right steel.'

Mace signalled to the potboy for another round. 'Why is it so busy this evening?'

'People have come up from the nearby villages. We're trying to decide if we're going to help that Black Talahan or not.'

'I think you should,' Irion said.

'Easy enough for you to say, you're just passing through,' Quiet Arthur replied. 'We know what Veng can do. Whole towns turned to Wolfheads for her army. The King's dead, Queen Zaphron's absent. People are scared.'

He was right, it was none of her business. Irion sat back and found Little Evelyn giving her one of those looks.

'When Quicky came to fetch us we had a conversation, him, me, Brian and the lad. We came back up to the keep because no matter what, we're the Blades and you and Mace were there.' The potboy delivered the fresh round, Evelyn helped herself to a mug and took a long pull. 'We thought we were going to stay.'

The pot boy cleared away the empties, Bobbins left his drink untouched and got up to help, moving between the tables and benches with practiced ease. Brian slid into his seat, saw the unclaimed tankard and drank half of it in a gulp. 'You should see what she's doing back there. So much with so little. Real talent, and a love for it too. I gave her my recipe for Winston O'Leary's hotpot du jour.'

Mace was amazed. 'You did? Really?'

'We cooks stick together.'

'Are we going to buy horses?' Bobbins asked Mace the following morning.

'We are not,' Mace said. 'It would take all our remaining money, and then they would die in the high passes.'

Brian was in the kitchen, Evelyn and Quicksilver were – somewhere. Bobbins combed the hay out of his hair with his fingers, dusted himself down, then took himself down the ladder to find Brian.

Irion sat with her feet hanging in space above the stalls, above the horses, plaiting three pieces of hay together. 'I like it here.'

'Grud, don't say that,' Mace said as she sat down beside her.

'I just did. Mace, look at the place, it's peaceful, prosperous, quiet. There are little temples and alters to more gods and godlings than you can shake a stick at, without prejudice. The king –' Irion caught herself, 'The *late* king even paid for a hospital. It's obvious he l–'

'Don't.' Mace cut the air with her hand. 'Don't use the "L" word. Just don't.'

'Liked. I was going to say liked. And the population *liked* him back, all right? I have the feeling Zaphron was cut from the same cloth. She would have made a good queen.'

'She probably would, but this isn't our fight,' Mace said.

'We can't run forever.'

Mace thought they could. 'We made a promise to Blackhart, to take him home.'

'When did he ever keep a promise himself?'

'Doesn't matter. We hold ourselves to our own standards.'

'I agree.'

Mace opened her mouth then closed it again. It had been a good while since Irion had out-reasoned her and it irritated her, though right then she couldn't work out who it was she was irritated at, or why. She took a blanket, climbed down the ladder and went out through the stables into the rocky lane. This high in the mountains it was always chilly in the mornings; she wound the blanket over her shoulders like a cloak and walked until her irritation passed and she could think again. They had come to Zangomar thinking it would offer a safe, if extended, route through the mountains and beyond. Then, in a land still far away, beneath a certain tree on a certain hill, they would lay Dante Blackhart to rest. Duty done.

None of this was what she had expected: the palace intrigue, Talahan's determination, the ghost queen. She wanted to tell herself it wasn't any of their business, not their fight, not their home. But she couldn't, not quite. *We can't run forever,* Irion had said.

A small stream cut across the path, fast and cold. Off to one side a dark-haired girl of five or six years filled a cracked cup from the babbling water and carried it up to an area of flat, bare rock. Mace sat away to one side and watched as, with infinite care, the girl dribbled water into a thin crevice in the bare rock. Curious, Mace came closer. The girl wore a ragged-hemmed dress and a threadbare shawl. Bare-legged, her feet were wrapped in rag shoes laced to wooden soles. Growing in the crevice was a rowan seedling with six small leaves. Already its twig of a trunk was woody, and although the divided leaves were wind-browned at the edges, a fat new bud had formed at the top of the stem.

'It's chosen a difficult place to grow,' Mace said.

The young girl said nothing until she'd finished pouring all the water into the crevice. 'It had no choice, but I can choose to help it grow.'

Struck by the young girl's conviction, Mace had a vision of the tree growing to maturity. Each year leaf litter gathered here and there; birds came to eat the berries; here and there more saplings grew into more trees. Under them, the children and grandchildren of this young scrap lived and played.

'Do you come here every day?'

'Yes.'

The girl stashed the cracked cup in its place beside the stream then went back to her chores in her home. Mace sat on the flat rock and watched the shadows move as the sun rose behind the mountains. A goatherd passed by, driving his goats towards pasture. One of the kids strayed up onto the rock and, before she even thought about it, Mace steered it back towards its herd before it saw the girl's little tree.

The goatherd raised his stick once and carried on. Mace looked back at the speck of green in the bare rock and shook her head.

When she was ready, she went back to the inn. Everyone else was there, and breakfast was waiting, a porridge of oats, fresh berries and wild honey. She sat down, took a bowl and began to eat. 'Blackhart would laugh in our faces. He'd call us babies and idiots.'

'Yes, he would,' Irion agreed. 'But he's not here, and we don't have to be the Blackhart Blades.'

'Who, then?'

'Anyone we damned well please.'

Little Evelyn sat back and folded her arms. 'Then I say from now on we're Irion's Blades.'

'Yes,' Quicksilver said.

Brian gently bumped his fist on the rough table. 'Irion.'

'All right,' Mace said. 'I'm in.'

At the end of the table, Bobbins managed the unusual trick of both hugging his knees and looking as if he might levitate from sheer joy.

They settled their account with the innkeeper then pooled what remained of their money on the table.

'How many goats do you reckon we can buy with that?' Irion said.

Brian swept half the coins into his hand. 'I can get us a deal.'

Two

Returning to the keep felt oddly like coming home. One of the guards raised her hand in greeting, Talahan came in from the work on the wall and leaned against the side of the cookhouse winding and unwinding the thread of a plumb-line around his finger.

'That's a lot of goats.'

'They're for you,' Irion said. 'Now you can sort out that spell of yours and get Zaphron back.'

'No, I've told you I can't. My troops, the wall –'

'You can leave all that to us now.'

Talahan closed his eyes and for a moment Irion saw the deep weariness there. 'I wanted to ask you to stay, I just never...' He shook away the thought, 'I can't offer you a quarter of the kingdom's wealth, but you will have a captain's pay, a warm bunk, and good food.'

'We'd like to prepare our own food. No offence, but we have a cook.'

'It would be nice to have a proper kitchen again,' Brian said, peering into the cookhouse. 'Do I have to share?'

'Probably.'

'Well, that's not going to work.'

Irion looked to the skies and muttered, 'Give me strength.'

'Brian can be in charge of the kitchen,' Talahan conceded. 'What's for supper?'

'Mimsy perigore a la grongules.' Brian dreamily fingered the knives in his bandolier. 'a.k.a. "Restronguet".'

'Oh, good,' Talahan looked puzzled. 'Family favourite.'

Talahan had organised his people well and Irion soon found the main improvement she could bring to his method was the extra pairs of hands in her troupe.

Two curtain walls ran across the valley from the keep to the gorge where the seething white waters of the Skrune plunged down. Each, when fully raised, would be twenty feet high, and buttressed with two small towers in the middle, and a larger one at the gorge end. Rather than try to repair both walls, Talahan used the masonry from the rear one to repair the outer. Irion continued the work, and also set a team to back-fill the wall gate with rubble.

'It's a weak point, and we're not going to be using it, are we?'

Zangomar's little army worked with quiet determination and the work proceeded well. Mace, Quicksilver, Little Evelyn and Bobbins each joined one of the teams of three and four Talahan had arranged. Irion joined in where extra help was needed, lifting fallen stones, placing and mortaring, and infilling the gap between the inner and outer faces with rubble. It was heavy, exhausting work.

Meanwhile, Talahan experimented with his magic. First, he carried a bench and stool, scrolls, paper, and ink down from his workroom to the main courtyard, then he roped off an area large enough to safely work. Finally, he tethered one of the goats to an iron post he had driven into the middle of the clear ground, where it placidly chewed on a heap of green scraps from the cookhouse.

After an hour's contemplation, reading, and note-making, Talahan cast his spell, thirteen syllables that clung to the air like treacle and set the teeth on edge. The goat briefly rippled, as might a reflection on water, then disappeared. Talahan made a note, then held his palms in front of his chest, a few inches apart, and *twisted*.

The goat reappeared, still placidly chewing, moving its jaw first to the left, then to right, apparently none the worse for wear.

Brian, who had come out of the cookhouse, watched from what he hoped was a safe distance. 'Is that it? You've fixed it?'

'No, that's what is supposed to happen, a correct casting, what I should have done. Invisibility, and then the dismissal.' Talahan made another note on his parchment. 'Now for the tricky part.'

All through the morning Talahan tried slight variations of the spell. He went slowly and carefully, sometimes with calculations in between, sometimes sitting motionless, lost in thought for minutes at a time. The different placement or utterance of those strange syllables briefly blurred the vision of anyone who came close, or gave them a deep if transient sense of profound unease, but each time it was the same, nothing happened, nothing at all.

Except once, when a goat blinked from view, reappeared, blinked away again, and proceeded to appear and disappear continually. Talahan wrote and drew diagrams for a long time, his mouth twisted in concentration, then led the creature away to one side and fetched another.

Talahan continued to study, and cast, and sometimes slowly walk beside the growing wall before returning to his stool.

Then came a bang, a pulse of red mist, a high-pitched scream. Talahan stood immobile with shock and covered in blood, in entrails, in small dripping bits of goat. Brian ran from the cookhouse, saw the state of him and led Talahan to a bench and sat him down. Not wanting to leave the mage, Brian called for a blanket, a cloth, a pail of water, and set two of the cookhouse crew to cleaning up with mops and brooms.

Brian soaked the cloth and wiped Talahan's face. 'It's all right. You're all right.' He picked gobbets of unknown parts of goat from Talahan's hair.

Huddled in the blanket, Talahan seemed incapable of speech. Brian sat beside him and watched the cleanup. Horns, bones, teeth and flesh, the goat had been diced more finely than he could have managed with his own knives. It had almost been *pureed*. Talahan blinked slowly and gave a great shudder. He took the cloth and washed his face, then sluiced his hands and arms clean.

Someone brought him a mug of water. Blank-eyed, Talahan rinsed, spat, then poured the rest over his head. Although he gulped and swallowed and worked his mouth, he still did not speak.

'Bring him some ale, spiced and hot,' Brian said. 'Bring me one too.'

Talahan held the mug in both hands, sipped, then drank slowly and steadily. When he was done Brian gave him his own untouched mug. 'An unpleasant shock, it's over now.'

'You don't understand,' Talahan croaked. 'That spell, as I spoke, I knew it was dimensionless.' He groped in his pocket for a coin and tossed it. 'The chances of it affecting me or the goat are just like that – blind luck.'

Now Brian felt some of Talahan's terror. He took his mug back from Talahan's unresisting hands and took a long drink himself.

Talahan roused himself. 'I have to make notes, I have to –' He gave Brian a ghoulish leer of a smile. 'No need to make the same mistake twice.' His hand shook as the quill scratched across the blood-soaked parchment. 'I have to –'

Brian took the quill from his fingers and laid it down. 'I think that's enough for today.'

Everyone felt better after a meal of braised trout stuffed with lemon and dill, served with new potatoes, samphire and individual crusty white loaves. As always, Brian served a meal fit for a prince, this time to all the men and women of the keep. The general mood visibly improved.

'What are "Grongules"?' Bobbins said as he mopped his plate with the last of his bread.

'Ay, well, grongules was off. Sorry about that,' Brian said.

'Well, the mimsy perigore were nice,' said Talahan, who had bathed and changed and was much more himself.

'Thank you,' Brian said. 'My own recipe.'

'May I ask, where did you manage to find –?

Mace stopped Talahan with a hand on his arm. 'We're just grateful to have a cook as fine as Brian.'

After the meal the Blades got together around a skin of decent red wine. Irion pulled off her long boots and sat with her feet towards the fire. 'So, how are we going to do this?'

Talahan looked around and kept his voice low. 'I don't see how we can win, so I want to make sure we don't lose.'

'And how do we do that?' Mace said.

'We make it expensive.'

'Veng won't care, she has a million men.'

'That doesn't matter here, there's no room for them to fight. If she sends that many most of them will sit miles behind the front line and she'll still have to feed and water them.'

Bobbins thought that sounded like good news. 'So how many will she send?'

'No more than ten thousand.'

'Oh.'

Talahan laughed silently. 'The keep and thirty determined men can hold against numbers like that for a year. It's been done before.'

Mace took the wineskin. 'If I were Veng I'd knock down the wall, ignore the keep, and move on.'

'That's why the wall has to hold.'

'I hear you have a few good tricks with walls.'

'That will buy us some time, no more.'

They began to talk over their assets.

'Quicksilver can put an arrow through the eye of a dog at three hundred feet,' Little Evelyn said. 'Except... It's just that the thing is...'

'The thing is, it's just dogs,' Quicksilver said. 'And I like dogs.'

'Marvellous.' Talahan smiled up at the sky and clasped his hands. 'You've all been touched in one way or another, haven't you? Cursed, or blessed.'

Irion couldn't deny it.

'Like Brian says, curses and blessings are not that different anyway,' Mace said. 'And not Bobbins, he's just joined us.'

Talahan lifted the wine skin in salute. 'An optimist. I can respect that.'

Quicksilver looked down at his leg. 'I make up for it. I've been cursed enough for two.'

The first sign of Veng's approach was a sudden influx of high valley farmers and herders, many driving their stock before them.

Then, a dark line appeared at the mouth of the valley. Hair-thin at first, it thickened as it came closer, the air above it grey with the dust of thousands of marching feet.

Talahan took one look then went back to experimenting with his goats.

Bobbins stood on the wall and stared and stared. Little Evelyn climbed up alongside him. 'This your first fight?'

Bobbins swallowed, then nodded. 'Talahan doesn't seem bothered at all.'

'He's probably thinking there's no point worrying about things you can't affect. He's right. Also, there's still plenty to do.'

'I know. I can't help it.'

'Do you want some tips?'

Bobbins turned and stood against one of the shoulder-high crenellations. 'Yes, please.'

'Rule number one: don't die.'

'Got it.' Bobbins swallowed again. 'Rule number two?'

'That's it, really. You don't have to kill them, just put them out of the fight. Of course, if they really are trying to kill you, then—' Evelyn made twisty stabbing motions with her hand.

'Kill them back?'

'That's the one.' Evelyn squeezed his shoulder. 'You'll be fine. Come one, let's get back to work.'

'Evelyn... May I ask about Quicksilver's leg?'

Evelyn looked around, then sat down. 'What is it?'

'It seems an amazing thing to me, so why is it a curse?'

'There's no magic where I come from, so when I first saw it I thought it was a wonder. It still is, but then I realised there's always some kind of price to pay with things like that. Even the simple spells Talahan casts, if nothing else they change him, and they change everyone else's attitude towards him. Respect, yes, but there's fear and distrust too. That's why you'll never see a mage rule a kingdom, or lead an army.

'Quicksilver did the Mer-folk a great favour, defeating Kane, the shark-who-walks, but losing his foot to Kane's bite in the process. In gratitude the Mer made him a better one, but every time he uses it, the Mer-metal creeps a little further up his leg.'

Veng's army occupied the valley a mile from the keep, where the valley floor lay wider and the Skrune flowed more placidly. Almost immediately, a team of engineers escorted by five hundred spears approached. Working with pickaxes and mauls, they set up a dozen twenty-foot-high wooden spikes, then withdrew.

That night Mace led a group of volunteers over the wall, knocked down the spikes, stacked them, poured oil, and set a fire that burned them to ash.

The next morning Veng's entire army advanced half way to the ash heap. This time Veng's engineers set up two hundred spikes.

Little Evelyn laughed, but she shivered too. 'That's literally overkill. Do you think they know how few of us there are?'

Mace studied the massed ranks of Veng's army through narrowed eyes. 'They don't need to.'

'So, then,' Irion said. 'Tomorrow?'

Mace nodded. 'Tomorrow.'

That day they finished the work on the wall, though the mortar was still wet and the middle towers were still low. In the evening Brian served a peppered goat stew swimming with dumplings, carrots, butter beans and fresh leeks.

'What do you call this one?' Talahan asked.

Brian paused in his eating, his spoon halfway between bowl and mouth. 'Goat stew.'

'Well, it's very good.'

Compliments flowed in from the other benches: 'Thank you, Brian,' 'Very good, Brian,' and, 'Is there any more?'

'The finest compliment of all,' Brian said, and he and Bobbins took the cook pots around the tables and ladled out extra portions to those who pushed their bowls forward.

The sun set in a cloudless sky. As colour faded from one horizon to the other stars appeared one by one, then in tens and dozens. Soon the night sky glittered with the bright constellations. Everything was cleaned away and tidied, and watchmen patrolled the wall. Talahan sat with the Blades around the fire in what was fast becoming a tradition, passing a wine skin back and forth.

Nobody had much to say. They had done what they could and tomorrow brought whatever tomorrow would bring. When the skin came back to Talahan for the second time he held it in in his hand for a moment. 'Well,' he said, before taking a swallow, 'I think I've worked it out, but there's a problem.'

'Of course there is,' Irion said.

Talahan had worked and studied all day, one cautious step at a time. Somewhere in between the correct casting of Phandaal's Temporary Vanishing, the near-lethal disaster of his random explosive disappearance spell, and the flickering goat, lay the casting he sought.

The hours went by and Talahan made no progress beyond using up all the parchment he had brought from his room. Over in the corner a goat still blinked into invisibility and back again. Tetchy with the long hours of study and the fear of creating some other lethal variant, Talahan raised his hand to dismiss the spell. Then he noticed the goat was not so much disappearing, as pausing. It raised a leg and vanished, and when it reappeared the leg was still raised. The animal was not becoming invisible, it was taking little jumps forward in time through an interval of nothingness of the same duration.

Talahan watched, awed and amused that he had created such a powerful yet ludicrous spell. It gave him ideas and he rifled through pages and pages of notes then sat in deep thought. Almost as an afterthought, he dismissed the spell on the goat and returned it to normal.

After two more attempts his heart thumped and his hand shook and he knew he had it. His mind brimmed with magic. Every scrap of parchment was covered in notes and diagrams. Although there was more in his room, he dared not wait, so he pushed back his gown sleeve and wrote the spell on the cuff of his white linen shirt.

Now Talahan understood the variant of the spell he had cast he could dismiss it at will, but that would not help Queen Zaphron, who was still in Steynhylda castle and at Banacort's mercy. Somehow they needed to send her a message.

Straightaway, Bobbins said, 'I'll go.'

It made sense. He knew the castle intimately and everyone else was obviously not from Zangomar. Mace bent down and pulled the dagger from her left boot. It was a double-edged thing with a seven-inch blade of old grey steel and a wire-wrapped handle. She offered it to Bobbins.

He reached for it, clearly wanting it, then took back his hand. 'Actually, I think I'll be better off without it. If I go in as a potboy and I'm searched they'll know I'm up to no good if they find something like that.'

Mace held the blade for a moment, then flipped it and returned it to her boot. 'It's yours when you return.'

'My spell displaced Zaphron in time. Not forwards, nor back, but *sideways,*' Talahan explained. 'A loop that folds back on itself, so she'll know neither extreme hunger nor thirst, but it also means she'll never see the sun set, when, technically, the spell would automatically expire.'

'All right,' Bobbins said, who struggled with the idea of anything moving sideways in time and had barely listened to the rest. 'What do you want me to do?'

'Take her this note.' Talahan held out a scrap of vellum. 'I've placed a glamour on it, a partial essence of the casting. It will make it easier for her to read, but harder for you to carry.'

Bobbins tried to take the vellum, but it slipped through his fingers like it was made of mist. He concentrated, and tried again, and this time he had it.

'You must always keep the vellum in your mind, or you will lose it. Can you do that?'

'Yes,' Bobbins promised. 'What if you did the same to one of my eyes, wouldn't that make it easier for me to find Queen Zaphron?'

Talahan thought about it. 'You're right, and I could, but then you would have two things to hold in your mind, and if you stopped thinking about your eye, well, you would drop that too.'

'Oh,' Bobbins said, and decided he would manage without. Having been working in Brian's kitchen, he needed little by way of disguise – a borrowed apron, an old piece of rag for a hood, a dusting of wood ash on his cheek. He set off an hour before dawn, when the first light appeared in the eastern sky. 'I'll be there in time to take up her breakfast tray. Nobody likes the job, too many steps, and there's Banacort's men.'

Talahan ordered the keep gates opened. Bobbins stood beside him, the vellum up his sleeve, one corner pinched between thumb and forefinger. He held a part of his attention fixed on the texture, the feel of the edge, the slight pressure of the material between the skin of his forearm and his sleeve.

'Look who's coming,' Mace said.

It was Bon Banacort himself, on a dun rouncey, dressed in the full panoply of his blue and red robes all stitched with silver thread under an ermine cloak. Looming behind him rode eight of his men, each in their black and shabby armour, on a mixture of hacks, stallions, and broomtails.

Talahan's hand came down on Bobbin's shoulder. 'Step aside, lad.' Bobbins found himself gently but firmly propelled into the shadows beside the gate.

'Sieur Bon Banacort, welcome to Hardknot Keep.' Talahan dipped his head and swept his arm in a movement that approximated a shallow bow. 'Veng the Usurper's army dips a toe into Zangomari lands and here you are riding to the kingdom's defence quicker than a kitten pounces on its own tail. I am impressed.'

Banacort looked down from his horse, his heavy chin doubled, his pebble eyes dark. 'Not quite in the manner you might expect, but yes, observant as ever, you have noticed I am here, come to put an end to this nonsense before things get out of hand.'

Irion could not help herself. 'What nonsense might that be?'

'Death, mayhem, failure. The placement of multiple fundaments on sharpened wooden poles.'

All around them the activity of Talahan's small army as it prepared for the coming day slowed, then ground to a halt. Men and women carrying stacks of spears, bundles of arrows, buckets of water, push-hooks, and barrows of unused masonry out along the wall stopped, turned back, and gathered around.

Off to the back and one side Mace spoke to Quicksilver in an urgent whisper. 'I would not ask this of you except now, in direst emergency. Hasten Bobbin's journey to the village and put him on a horse. Please.'

'It will cost me a full inch on my leg,' Quicksilver said. 'Maybe more.'

'It's either that or we run now. Banacort's tongue will turn these people and Talahan will stand alone. I – Please. My soul-sworn oath: I will never ask again.'

Quicksilver saw how Banacort had instinctively ridden in to occupy the centre of the courtyard, flanked by his men. Behind them the gate stood open and the road was clear. 'Very well.'

It was easy for Quicksilver to slip around the back of the gathered crowd unnoticed and lead Bobbins outside.

'Hold tight to my belt,' Quicksilver told Bobbins, and they were gone to the village in seven enormous springing jumps. Several villagers watched them arrive, astonished by the sight of two men seemingly dropping from the sky. Quicksilver gathered himself, doing his best to ignore the familiar grinding ache all around the seam of his leg where flesh met creeping metal. Beside him, Bobbins stood on knees half turned to water, gasping and blowing, dazzled by the speed and height of Quicksilver's leaps and more glad than he could describe that it was over.

Quiet Arthur came from the forge, his great hammer in his hand. 'We saw that Sieur Banacort pass by. If there's news, tell us.'

'Veng's Army is here and Talahan holds the keep.' Quicksilver slapped Bobbins on the shoulder, 'This lad needs a fast horse to Steynhylda.'

'My Jennet is quick, steady, and long-winded,' Arthur said. 'You can take her.'

Quicksilver watched Bobbins head off at a trot, then, when he reached better ground, a full gallop. He sat for a while and massaged his leg until the cold ache at his thigh faded to a duller agony.

'That leg of yours is something,' Arthur said.

'It's something, all right,' Quicksilver muttered.

'Will it take a mark, would you feel it?'

'Only as would bronze, and yes, like my own flesh.'

Arthur fetched two tin mugs of mint tea, steaming hot and sweet with honey. Holding the mugs in old rags they sipped and watched the day brighten. When he had finished Quicksilver thanked Arthur then limped the miles back to the keep.

As Quicksilver walked, a scrap of vellum blew and tumbled down the stairs of the peacock tower, across the drawbridge of Steynhylda castle, out along the High Street, down the Market Way and through the town gates. Avoiding ditches and puddles, moving against the prevailing wind, it danced and fluttered up along the valley road faster than a man could run. It blew past goatherds and running boys with cleft sticks, and through the village where Quiet Arthur worked and the potboy at the First and Last worked to clean up from the previous night's busy house of old men and women and strong sons and daughters.

The parchment blew all the way to Hardknot Keep, through the gate and up to the hall, where Brian served a slow but steady flow of supremely delicious breakfast dishes to Banacort and his men. Talahan sat with them and ate sparingly while he watched and waited. He snagged the scrap of vellum as it blew around his feet, made his excuses, and went to his room, leaving the door ajar.

He put the vellum onto the table and stood back.

'Queen Zaphron, are you here?'

The door swung and creaked, then slammed shut. The vellum fluttered up into the air, scrunched itself into a ball and flung itself at Talahan's head.

Talahan went over to where he had carefully hung yesterday's shirt, read what he had written on the cuff, and released his spell. Queen Zaphron appeared, insubstantial at first, as if made of fog, then as if she stood behind a flowing sheet of water. Finally she was herself, a young woman of average height, with mid-brown hair cropped to her jaw line. She wore a long-sleeved dress of deep green barragan cut into four calf-length panels at the waist, with dark leggings and grey boots beneath.

Immediately Talahan went to one knee. 'Majesty.'

'Oh, get up, you idiot,' Zaphron said.

Talahan regained his feet and for a long moment they regarded each other before slowly stepping forwards into an open embrace. Talahan drew back. 'I am so very sorry.'

Zaphron looked around the room, her expression drawn and tired. 'I don't know whether to thank you or hit you.' She fixed Talahan a steady look and he looked down. She punched him on the chest hard enough to stagger him.

'There was nothing there, Talahan. No living creature, no bird, no beast, just the lonely wind and the stones of Steynhylda castle, and sometimes a fire in the hearth.'

'I can only imagine how frightened you must have been.'

'That first time I noticed the sun was not going to set...' Zaphron's mouth twisted. 'It wasn't easy holding onto hope, holding onto trust. I thought you might have... done this on purpose. I was lonely, bored, and scared, it's a poor combination. I sang to keep my spirits up. I raided the kitchen but the food vanished in my mouth.'

'I made a mistake.' Talahan explained the fault with his spell. 'I didn't know what to do.'

'Sometimes I could hear voices, faint and distorted.' Zaphron took a deep breath. 'I believe Banacort works to betray us.'

'I believe so too.' Talahan outlined the situation with Veng, Banacort, and the keep. 'Since you have been... Elsewhen I have worked to achieve all we talked about. I also discovered Banacort secreted the treasury here, something that is now perhaps to our advantage. He's here, down in the hall with his thugs. Veng's army gathers, I have to go. What do you need?'

'Five minutes alone, then a strong drink and some company.'

'All of those I shall provide,' Talahan said. 'I'll ask Irion to come. She leads a curious troupe of vagabonds and I think you'll find her – interesting.' He made to depart, then turned in the door. 'You being here makes all the difference.'

Down in the hall Talahan poured two tankards of red ale and presented them to Irion. 'Take these up to my room. Someone is there in need of this. She will explain further.'

At the head of the table Banacort was deep in conversation with Brian. 'Those brandied ortolans were magnificent! And the little silver breaded fish, what did you call them again?'

'Krivens, smooshed with doofers.'

'Doofers, eh? Extraordinary! So savoury, yet lemony too. If I may say, next time perhaps a little more garlic.'

Little Evelyn stifled a snort of laughter by turning it into a cough.

'You must stay, of course.' Banacort wafted his hand, the gesture encompassing the keep, the valley, the entirety of Zangomar. 'When this little kerfuffle is over you must stay and cook for me. Of course you will.'

Brian looked down at his hands. 'Of course.'

Banacort glanced through the windows to check the sun and pushed back his chair. 'A splendid repast, but the day won't save itself.'

Out in the courtyard little progress had been made on any of the tasks Irion had set. Once again Banacort held forth to anyone who would listen while his men slouched watchfully here and there.

'People of Zangomar, we are challenged but I say we will endure. More than endure, we shall thrive. I am here, now, as herald of the dawn to a new era which shall begin thus: Primus, I confer with Veng or her ambassador; secundus, I present the gift I have prepared. Tertius, her armies withdraw to leave us in peace.'

Talahan's small army stood and listened, and if there was doubt in their eyes there was hope too. And still the wall stood undefended.

Banacort shrugged off his ermine cloak and lifted his hand to the sky.

'Such black shadows as lay 'pon the land,
And o'er minds and hearts, a dark caul of despair,
Now blow and dissipate like wind-blown sand,
Eyes lift in hope where fingers once clutched hair.
As, striding forth, staff and sword upraise-ed,
A new dream begins, a new day.

Hope. Hope. Hope, which sets all hearts a-thunder.
Reluctant comes the hero, but come he still, and I am—'

Zaphron's raised voice cut through Banacort's declamations. 'Thank you, Sieur Bon Banacort, none of that will now be necessary.'

Standing beside her, Irion expected the ordinary people of Zangomar to kneel, or perhaps cheer, but to her amazement none of them did. Instead, after a moment of amazed delight, they applauded. And although she had only known Zaphron for the few minutes they had drunk together and talked, she had begun to understand why. Her cold hands lifted of their own accord and, somewhat self-consciously, she applauded too. Somewhere nearby she was convinced Mace was laughing at her, but when she looked, she found that big bold warrior leaning against the forge wall, arms folded, with a big grin on her stupid lovely battered face. Irion found herself grinning too, and blinked hard, and then a few times more.

Banacort's own face flushed white with shock, then turned dark puce as his fingers splayed and clutched at nothing. 'My queen, why, praise be, how all the gods have blessed us. In our hour of need you are here, and you are safe, you are well!'

'No thanks to you. You think I don't remember?'

'A-ha,' Banacort gulped, 'A precaution, your safety, er... paramount concerns.'

'Listen, everyone,' Zaphron declared. 'Bon Banacort stole our collective wealth and tried to have me killed. He is here now to sell us to Veng.'

The courtyard grew very still, and very quiet.

An archer called down from the wall. 'Is this true?'

'To save you, to keep us safe,' Banacort pleaded.

'To save yourself, to keep your position safe,' Zaphron growled.

'My dearest queen, I would never –'

'Out of my sight, Banacort, I am sick of your duplicity and lies. Sieur no longer.'

Banacort opened his mouth then found Little Evelyn right beside him, and between them in her hand was a very sharp and pointy knife, the tip just pricking under his ribs.

'Shame, that. You almost had me going. "Reluctant comes the hero," and all that. Let's sit down, shall we?'

'Men,' Banacort squeaked. 'To me?'

The only part of Banacort's men that moved were their eyes as each took in the archers on the wall, the two score determined spears in the courtyard, and Irion's Blades, all with weapons drawn. Then Talahan swept his hands into an extravagant gesture, a clear and obvious precursor to casting. The leader, a hulking scarred brute of a man, hooked his thumbs through his belt, well clear of his scabbard. 'Escort duty only.'

'Escort duty, you duplicitous shit?' Banacort spluttered. 'I don't pay you just for escort duty.'

The sell-sword gave an indifferent shrug. 'That's what you said when you kicked us out of warm beds an hour before sunrise.'

'A figure of speech! Come now, this is urgent!'

'Sounds like you didn't get your Tees and Cees in writing,' Evelyn laughed. 'Always a good idea when contracting out,'

Banacort looked like he was about to lose his temper so she poked him with her knife and he started like a flushed hare. 'Come along, Mister Banacort, Sieur no longer, nice and easy does it.'

Evelyn led him over to the main gate, where he leaned for a moment, head in arms, before composing himself and straightening. 'My robe, would you mind?'

Evelyn retrieved his ermine cloak, he shrugged it on and huddled inside, defeated, confused, and completely at a loss. 'This is so unfair, I am the victim here. Always, I worked for Zangomar.' Tears lay on his cheeks but he did not wipe them away. 'Do tell, did you really like my verse?'

'No, you slimy twerp, it was rubbish.'

Banacort's face grew hard, his eyes like little beads of dark glass. 'You will end up sitting on one of Veng's spikes,' he hissed. Then he screeched back into the keep. 'On a big spike, every single one of you.'

'And I'll shank you up with my little one, right here, right now,' Little Evelyn whispered, her breath hot on his ear. 'So jog on, gobshite.'

Mace had fought in many battles and knew that most started reluctantly. The morning drew on, the sun rose higher and higher, the spears and armour of the massed ranks of Veng's army glittered like the sea on a clear day, but still they did not come.

Irion used the time well, ensuring all the preparations Banacort had interrupted were complete. Not one for grand speeches, she walked the wall and talked to everyone on watch, a word here, an adjustment of armour there. 'These walls are strong, they will hold, you built them well.'

Bobbins helped out in the courtyard, fetching and carrying, worrying that he had no armour and how he would do when the time came. Every now and then he took out the knife Mace had given him and turned it over in his hand.

'Nice little blade, that,' Evelyn said, appearing at his side. 'Know how to use it?'

'Not really.'

'Like this.' Evelyn stabbed him with two fingers in the stomach again and again, her elbow driving in and out, ten blows in three seconds. 'Stick them once they can still kill you. Do it like that and they stay dead.'

Bobbins grimaced queasily. 'All right.'

Queen Zaphron watched the encounter and when Evelyn was done she came over with a helmet and shield. 'The men and women on the wall are going to need water, bandages, and other help. I'm no more a warrior than you, but I can help others fight and I could use someone to protect me. Bobbins, will you be that person?'

Here was something Bobbins knew he could do, he felt his resolution form. 'I will.'

Soon after Banacort had departed, hastening away on the horse he had ridden in on, Talahan spoke to the leader of his men, the sell-sword Boland. All the others lingered, helping themselves to the uneaten leftovers from breakfast and asking, politely enough, if there was spare bread and meat for their saddlebags. Talahan let them have what he considered to be enough and no more, neither grudging it nor being over-generous.

Boland was like his men, pragmatic, amoral, and drawn to the easy life of wolves banding together for a safe kill. More certain of the answer than whether it was a good idea to ask the question in the first place, Talahan nevertheless went ahead: 'Will you fight for us here, on the wall? A half-ounce of gold per man per day.'

Boland ran his tongue along the edges of his teeth. 'Two days, today and tomorrow.'

The last thing Talahan wanted was a grim troop like Boland's pulling out halfway through the fight, it sent too clear a message. He said as much and doubled his offer.

'No, I don't think we will,' Boland said, and that was that. Talahan, truth be told, was relieved.

Boland drew his men together, they mounted, and rode out. Talahan walked through the gate to see them off and Boland reigned in his grey hack as he passed by.

'I hear the high passes are clear.'

Talahan saw no reason to dissemble. In his experience life had a way of bringing people around and back together again and those like Boland had long memories. 'They are, but sell your horses first. The high passes are just that, high. The cold and the dry will kill them.'

The corners of Boland's mouth twitched down, he jerked his head once, and kicked his horse on.

Nothing else happened that day. In the evening Mace, Irion and Talahan sat down to talk.

'They are either not ready, or they're playing games.' Irion's hand shook and she made a fist. 'They might be making siege engines.'

'There's no sign of that yet,' Talahan said. 'It's difficult to bring them up here.'

'Let's play a few games of our own,' Mace said. 'Light a hundred torches, make them worry we have an army.'

They did just that, and in the morning Veng's army came.

They came slowly and steadily, with shields and ladders, and archers behind. Talahan, who still had one more trick up his sleeve, kept watch from the keep and left the wall empty.

Irion and Mace each took one of the mid-wall towers and kept inside along with thirty men and women per tower.

Mace peered through an arrow slit and watched Veng's massed force approach. A thousand against the wall, an unknown number of archers, the main mass held back in reserve. This was a test, a probe. If it worked, it worked, and tonight Veng's troops would feast in the courtyard and drink from their skulls. Or not. Behind her, Talahan's men and women checked their kit again, and then again, tightening belts, loosening swords in scabbards, taking helmets off and on.

A hard clatter began on the roof and walls, sparse at first, like magpie feet as they picked moss from slates, then quickly built to a steady roar like hail – arrows in their hundreds, in their thousands, the hardest rain. They made the light change. Mace dropped down from the narrow window set the shutter in place. 'That's a lot of arrows, and to think we brought our own.'

That won her a couple of nervous smiles, a laugh from the boldest, pretending. For Mace it had never been a pretence. She was ready for this day, she relished it. She knew that fear was real because she saw it in others, in everyone else, but never in herself. She knew that on days like these, in the hours and the minutes and the fleeting moments between life and death, the brave overcame their fear and they stood and fought; which meant that everyone else, from Irion to Bobbins, from Talahan to Queen Zaphron, and the men and women with her now, all were braver than her. She thought it meant she had to try harder, and that was her curse.

'When this stops we are going outside,' Mace said. 'You are scared, I am scared, and believe me, the gods know we are. I know it because I know they are watching. And I know they are watching because we are about to do the one thing that they cannot. We are risking our lives, and it fascinates them, those immortals we pray to. You risk yours for the ones you love, for this country of yours, but most of all, when you are out on that wall, for the man or woman at your side.

'And me? I've had enough of running from Veng. Today you are my brothers and sisters and I stand with you. Now, let us ready ourselves.'

Mace went to them all in turn and gripped their shoulders. Most did the same back to her. A few of them prayed, one hurriedly turned away and vomited into a bucket.

A prayer and a puke and a mouthful of water, that was how these moments went.

The arrow storm died away.

'Come on.' Mace kicked open the door and ran out onto the wall, and knew, just knew, that they would follow.

A wall is a wall, low or high. If you see a high wall, you bring a longer ladder, and when you think you are close enough to the wall you set your ladder down. This time Talahan cast his illusion onto the ground so the wall appeared closer than it actually was.

Roaring and shouting, Veng's men ran forwards. Every single one of them set their siege ladders down too soon and they fell flat among the stones. As they ran to lift them again, Talan's little army rained down their own hail of arrows.

Now Veng's attackers set their ladders against the walls. Mace and Irion's squads heaved them aside with hooked poles. Ladders toppled, men fell, both lay broken. Veng's troops milled uncertainly under the wall taking flanking fire from the towers and keep but refusing to fall back.

They tried for a third time, piling onto the remaining ladders, their combined weight making them harder to dislodge. Silver ramshorns blew, clean and bright, and with a great howling cheer another five hundred ran forwards with more ladders, their shields over their heads. Behind them Veng's main army howled, and thundered their spears and swords against their shields.

Now the attack grew determined. Here and there, in their ones and twos, Veng's soldiers gained a foothold. Mace and Irion rushed squads up and down the wall and threw them back, but here and there, in their ones and twos, the Zangomari defenders cried out and staggered back, or silently dropped and lay still.

Talahan sent in half his reserve. Bobbins and Queen Zaphron ran crouched behind them, Bobbins held a shield over Zaphron and trusted to his helm and coat of fence. The walking wounded they stitched, or bandaged, or seared with the hot poker Bobbins carried in a bucket of coals. Their yells and screams joined the general hubbub, the stink of burnt flesh mixed with the sour metallic reek of sweat and blood, and worse. The badly hurt they helped into the towers and tended as best they could. The dead they rolled from the battlement path.

Quicksilver and Little Evelyn fought as a pair, sword and axe. With four others they cleared and held their part of the wall.

There came a time when the press grew desperate and for a long moment all that could be heard were the grunts and gasps of fighting men and women, the sounds of blade striking against blade, against armour, biting into flesh.

Then it was past. Veng's footholds on the wall were reduced and eliminated, and the ladders were down. Out on the stony field the ramshorns blew again. Veng's men retreated. There seemed little reason to cheer.

Quicksilver and Little Evelyn watched them go. Evelyn pointed to one of the ramshorns, closer than the rest. 'Think you can hit that?'

'I'll miss.'

'Give it a go.'

Quicksilver sighed and unslung his bow. He nocked an arrow, drew, and let fly. His aim was true, yet somehow, at the last moment the arrow drifted aside. It struck the silver ramshorn and knocked it from the player's grasp so its pure note squawked up the through the octaves. All along the wall Talahan's men and women laughed.

Evelyn clapped her hand on Quicksilver's shoulder. 'Good miss.'

That night torches burned along the wall and fires blazed in the courtyard. Beyond the back wall eighteen bodies lay wrapped in clean white linen.

Brian served a simple meal of rye bread, sausage and red beet and then, when all had eaten their fill, brought small dishes of a dark smooth paste, each with its own little spoon with a bowl no larger than a thumbnail.

'What's this, Brian?' Irion said.

'This,' Brian said, rubbing his hands, "Is twissany felpules sans oingles".' He nodded towards Evelyn. 'I've been saving this one.'

Evelyn dipped her spoon and tasted a tiny amount. Her eyes went wide, she took a full spoonful, closed her eyes and groaned with pleasure. 'Brian, is this *chocolate mousse?*'

'I've never tasted anything like it,' Irion said.

'It's amazing.' Bobbins said, and that was the general agreement. When he tried to help clean up in the kitchen Brian gently propelled him towards the door. 'Go and make the most of tonight.'

'Well, what about you?'

'I'm going to do just that.' Brian spread his arms. 'This is who I am, it's what I do.'

'You don't want some company?'

'Not tonight.'

Out in the courtyard Irion and Mace sat reminiscing with Talahan and Zaphron. Bobbins joined them and with no stories of his own to match theirs simply sat and listened.

'All done?' Mace said.

'Brian said I should make the most of the evening.'

'And so you should, so we all should,' Talahan said and a look passed between Irion, Mace, and himself.

Guards patrolled the wall in shifts. Here and there small groups gathered around fires, some talked, some sang low sweet songs while others sat quietly. Bobbins noticed some seeking out dark corners in the stables, behind the forge, mostly male and female, but not all. Seeing them made him wonder where Quicksilver and Little Evelyn were and he decided not to ask a foolish question.

'What about you, Bobbins?' Zaphron said.

Perhaps it was exhaustion and the aftermath of such a fearsome day, but in the low light Bobbins thought Zaphron had a beauty that came from something far more beautiful inside. And Mace seemed like a force of nature held constrained, while Talahan was a man of dread power and determination. As for Irion, he knew she was someone he would follow into all the hells and back.

'I'm happy to sit with you.'

'You sit,' Irion said emphatically, 'in the company of your peers.' She raised her tankard and everyone knocked them together, Bobbins last of all. Later, when he lay down to sleep, aching and bruised, so weary, and fearful of the coming dawn, he told himself that whatever the future held, he, Bobbins the orphan child, the reject from the king's kitchen, had lived that moment around the rough table. He had sat in the company of heroes and that could never be taken away.

The next dawn Veng sent her full army, a mass of creeping shield turtles. Among them rolled an enormous hollow wagon on ten iron-bound wheels, each wheel as tall as a man, with a steeply pitched roof covered in sopping wet hides. Inside it hung Veng's Tooth, a fifteen-tonne bronze battering ram, and fifty men to swing it.

Irion watched them come, and her shoulders drooped the tiniest fraction. 'Long day.'

Beside her, Mace nodded. She shielded her eyes. 'Wolfheads.'

Crouched behind the wall Little Evelyn started, took a look and laughed silently. 'You hear that, Quicksilver? Wolfheads.'

The Wolfheads. Veng's elite force, her army within an army that, until the ramshorns blew, would not take a single step back.

Quicksilver, who had not really been listening, merely grunted and continued sliding his whetstone along the edge of his sword.

Evelyn elbowed him in the ribs. 'Wolf's a kind of dog, innit.'

The steady scrape of the whetstone stopped as a slow light grew in Quicksilver's eye. For the first time since he'd been with the Blades, Bobbin saw Quicksilver's bare-toothed smile. It was something he hoped never to see again.

Quicksilver sheathed his sword and gained his feet. 'I'm going to need arrows, lots of arrows.'

Black Talahan smiled his blackest smile. 'Bring this man a barrel of clothyards.'

Quicksilver was already stringing his bow. 'Make it two.'

If there was only going to be one glory day then this was it. And if it belonged to any one person, it was Quicksilver.

Irion's plan to backfill the outer gate proved itself. Under a storm of fire-pots Veng's Tooth futilely battered the gate to splinters only to reveal the rubble-filled tunnel.

Meanwhile, Quicksilver was – everywhere. Running from tower to tower and along the walls between, constantly on the move, he let loose his own personal storm of arrows, and despite shield walls and helms, he did not miss, not once. Such a toll he took on the Wolfheads that at one moment the attack faltered, and seeing it, Quicksilver laughed.

Then he *danced*.

With a clutch of arrows in his hand Quicksilver flew from tower to tower, from tower to keep and back again. Spinning leaps carried him a hundred feet into the air. Down below, Wolfsheads fell, and they fell. Arrows arced up towards him but he was always gone, down to the wall for more arrows and up again, a leap, a turn, a laugh, and Wolfheads died.

Protected by its wagon, Veng's Tooth began a ponderous retreat. Although the roof was covered in wet hides burning oil from the fire-pots had caught here and there and one of the heavy wooden wheels was firmly ablaze.

Quicksilver dropped down beside it, let loose a flurry of arrows, then leapt to the wall and back down on the other side. Inside the wagon Wolfheads staggered and died, pinned to the oaken frame. The wagon, without enough crew to push it, ground to a halt. Soon it began to burn in earnest.

Out in the stony field a Wolfhead mage, collared and chained, clapped their hands, raised their arms, and cast a spell of twenty-three syllables so unnatural that they would not fit into a normal person's throat. In front of them the ground leapt away in a running furrow, arrow-straight and arrow-fast towards the wall where Quicksilver stood, scattering stone and men and Wolfheads as it went.

In one smooth motion Quicksilver raised his bow and aimed high. Then the wall beneath him burst apart and he tumbled down. Wolfheads surged in, howling and stabbing as they clambered over the rubble, over Quicksilver, and into the breach.

Even as this happened, even as the Wolfhead mage stood looking, Quicksilver's arrow arced down and struck them through the eye, and they fell.

Here was the pivot of the day. While everyone else stood frozen with despair, Irion strode forwards and stood like a bulwark and broke all who came against her. Then Little Evelyn flung herself forwards, screaming, an axe in each hand, and stood beside her.

And Brian the Knifewife came. Still wearing his cook's apron, he simply walked into the expanding seethe of Wolfheads. His hands wove a knife-pattern so fast the blades were a flickering steel blur, cutting, chopping, slicing, dicing, and everyone he touched died. On his flank came young Bobbins, who hacked and slashed with some notched and discarded sword and half-shattered shield.

Behind them Talahan drew up his reserves, thirty archers, who sent volley after ragged volley into the breach. Soon the Wolfheads clambered and slipped over their own rolling, sliding dead. But still they came.

Talahan, half in despair, flung off his cloak, drew his own sword and rushed forwards. With him came the remaining men and women of Hardknot Keep, a shield-wall just two bodies deep folding around the breach. One end anchored itself against the rubble where Quicksilver lay, the whole line pushing and stamping, swords stabbing between shields as they heaved and shoved their way towards Irion, who still stood.

Still the Wolfheads came, and although the shield wall held, the Wolfheads fell on its flank, forcing a gap between them and Irion and her few Blades.

Then Mace was there, a force of nature. And if Irion was the bulwark, then Mace, with her two-handed sword, was the grim hurricane. Not one step back, the Wolfheads' reputation held, but faced with Mace's furious upswing and downstroke, left and right, they fell where they stood.

Into the space behind Mace came Irion and the Blades, a fighting wedge, driving forwards. Seeing them, Talahan took heart and as the sun dipped towards the horizon he called a final order. The archers dropped their bows, seized their spears and hurled themselves forwards.

Shield wall and spear fence encircled the Wolfheads and ground them down. In the lowering twilight Mace achieved the breach with Irion at her side. With the rest of the Blades they threw all who still came at them down to ruin. Then every Wolfhead behind them was dead and a hundred spears and shields massed in the breach. Wolfheads came until the sun set and the silver ramshorns blew and what was left of them melted away.

Under a golden red sky undershot by drifting smoke Mace climbed one side of the breach, her black silhouette outlined by the flames of Veng's blazing wagon. Reaching the top, she thrust up her sword and gave a great shout. Down below it was answered, for this time the Blades and the army of Zangomar had something to shout about.

Quicksilver lay on the ground, his head cradled in Little Evelyn's lap. Blood and air bubbled on his chest with every breath.

Mace knelt beside him. 'Help is coming, very soon.'

Quicksilver nodded and closed his eyes.

Bobbins stared at the mer-metal, which now enclosed Quicksilver's entire leg and one side of his body to his ribs, and whispered, 'What happens when it reaches his heart?'

'He's more worried about what happens when it reaches his cock,' Evelyn said, but she was weeping.

Quicksilver coughed and swallowed. 'You're the one should worry.'

'Promises, promises,' Evelyn leaned down and kissed his brow.

Quicksilver cleared his throat, and again. There was more blood, bright on his teeth. Evelyn smoothed his hair, he reached for her hand and she held his tight. He looked up into her eyes and smiled, and relaxed. And just like that, just as he had always done, Quicksilver was gone.

An hour later Irion and Talahan stood at the breach and looked out across the stony land towards Veng's army a half-mile distant. Talahan held a large clay pot in his hand, its shoulders dusty and cobwebbed, the neck sealed with old black wax. He wiped away the dust, knocked off the top of the neck against the broken wall and drank. He passed the bottle to Irion, who discovered the pot held brandy, old, strong and rich. Feeling the warmth of it glow in her stomach, she said as much. Talahan, looking into the night, said, 'Just how I like my women.'

Irion snorted and they passed the pot back and forth.

A hundred yards in front of the gate the wagon of Veng's Tooth still burned, a mass of charred beams and glowing embers.

Irion shivered and rubbed her hands together. 'That looks cosy.' Talahan drank and considered the comment as if it was something serious and sensible.

'Why not.'

They picked their way towards the smouldering wreck, found a place close enough to feel the warmth, and sat with their backs against a boulder. For a while neither of them spoke, then Talahan said, 'I was born here. My family has a farm up in the far hills, way past Steynhylda.'

Realising this was the start of a confession, Irion said nothing.

'I was a fool of a young man, more than a fool.' Talahan stared at his feet. 'I brought shame on my parents and the day came when I realised what I had done and I felt that shame too. Rather than try to make amends I took myself away and never came back. By then people were calling me Black Talahan and it stuck. No matter where I went and what I did that name followed me, and I felt I deserved it.

'Then, by chance, I met Zaphron on her travels. I'd been away so long I thought I could never return, and all the amends I'd spent the rest of my life trying to make were done in other cities, other countries. She told me that everything I'd done had been forgiven and forgotten, and persuaded me to come back with her.' Talahan took a swallow of brandy. 'So I did.'

'Do you parents still live?'

'They are old, but they do, yes.'

'Have you seen them?'

Talahan hung his head. 'No.'

A flickering yellow light picked its way towards them through the wreckage of the battlefield and resolved into Bobbins carrying a hooded lantern. Irion handed him the clay pot, which still held an inch of brandy. Bobbins drained it, put it down carefully, and took a breath. 'You need to come and see this.'

Back through the breach Talahan and Irion saw a body of men and women up from the villages, a hundred strong. Quiet Arthur stood at their head, his blacksmith's hammer over his shoulder. Many had already spread out to tend the wounded troops, and behind them a procession of torches still wound up along the valley road.

'We don't know how to fight,' Quiet Arthur said, 'But we heard our queen was here. What can we do?'

For a moment Talahan could not speak, then he showed Arthur the breach in the wall. 'Can you raise that by morning?'

Quiet Arthur called two masons over, who looked, and stuck out their jaws, and finally nodded. 'Consider it done.'

Overnight Veng's army was reinforced, a black river that swept away into the distance. The next morning Veng herself walked out into the dead space between her army and the wall. She was accompanied by two warriors, one who moved like a mountain, and one who slunk along like a whip. She led a collared mage tethered to a chain in her hand.

A dozen of her knights set up pennants of gold-trimmed red then put down a small square table. They unfolded and spread a cloth of the same material over it and withdrew a hundred paces.

Talahan watched the activity then looked around at the mountains, the keep, the people of Zangomar behind him, and felt he was seeing everything properly for the first time. He turned to Queen Zaphron. 'I can only see one way out of this, and it's a wild and dangerous chance.'

Zaphron listened, then called Irion's Blades over. Talahan repeated his proposition. 'Irion, will you come with me?'

'We all will,' Irion said.

Talahan went to his room and put on his old shirt, then carefully and with great fear studied another spell until it hung clear in his mind.

Veng the Usurper sat waiting for them in her campaign chair, sipping a green tea she poured from a steaming golden carafe. A plate of sweet yellow crackers lay untouched in front of her. She seemed thoroughly at ease. Behind her stood her two warriors, one still as a mountain, the other like the grass in a breeze. The tethered mage crouched at her feet like a beaten dog.

She stood as they approached, and Talahan saw a rather short, somewhat plump middle-aged woman, her mouse-brown hair held in circlet of white gold. She wore an eagle-patterned ankle-coat of black and silver lampas with a high collar and deep buttoned cuffs over a lavender silk blouse, white trousers, and knee boots.

He also saw the rings on her fingers and pendant at her throat, recognising them for the power items they were.

Veng looked over her shoulder at the hundred spikes set in the ground, then sat again in the only chair. She sipped her tea, she scratched at the corner of her eye and sighed. 'This only ends one way. I decide who lives and dies, I decide who comes and goes.'

'Why have you come here?' Talahan said.

'I grew weary of my husband's treachery and tired of the lies kings tell.'

'Why have you come *here*?' Talahan repeated.

'Where is the archer who killed so many of my Wolfheads?'

'He died.'

'Just as well,' Veng said, then spoke to her tethered mage. 'Tell me about these people.'

The mage rose, cast his gaze over them, indicated Bobbins and spoke in a low whisper. 'Two days ago this one was an ordinary boy. Now he is a man.

'This one is cold; this one lives without fear; this one is Brian the Knifewife and he is peerless; this one is the queen of her realm and the last of her line; this one is —' His eyes on Little Evelyn, the mage faltered. 'This one harks not from this world or any other known to me and I would speak with her further.'

'I allow it,' Veng said. 'You, I reprieve. The rest of you die today. Your final free choice is which spike you will sit upon. Defy me and every man and woman in Zangomar joins my Wolfheads, their children starve, and Zangomar ceases to exist.' She turned to the last of them, Talahan. 'Who is this?'

'This is Talahan, who once styled himself 'The Black' for a guilt now redeemed. He is a magus of limited reach, and he holds a killing spell in his mind.'

Veng looked disappointed. 'I allow no unshackled magic in my lands.'

Talahan smiled. 'Then the wizards of Kelophase still hold.'

Anger flickered over Veng's brow like summer thunder. 'For now.'

'Leave us be,' Zaphron said. 'We acknowledge you as Empress of the Known World, we are no threat.'

Veng smiled. 'When I began I made myself a promise. "Empress of the World excepting little Zangomar," lacks a certain cachet, don't you think? Behind me lies peace. Surrender, and your people will enjoy the same, even though you cannot.'

'We had peace,' Talahan said. 'Until you came.'

Veng sat for a while, her hands flat on the table. Then her fingers began to drum. 'Take that spell from Talahan and cast it against him.'

'No.' Bobbins started forwards but Mace's outflung arm blocked him. Talahan stood like an iron rod, his fists clenched at his sides.

The shackled mage folded his palm over his fist, jerked his hands apart and Talahan staggered. The mage spoke thirteen wrenching syllables, and then disappeared in a sudden, shattering burst of gore, bone and flesh.

Veng's two guards were down. The quick one with one of Evelyn's axes through his knee, the other in his skull; the great one clubbed down by the rock in Irion's hand.

He was down but not out. Bobbins thought of Quicksilver and a coldness came over him. His knife hand was like a piston, driving, and although the huge warrior regained his feet it was only to fall again, and Bobbin's sleeve was red to the elbow.

Veng's twelve men at arms rushed forwards. Mace stepped into their path and drew her long sword. 'Who will die?' Their charge faltered, though three came on, and although Mace took wounds to her right arm and leg, all three fell. She settled her stance. 'Who will die?'

Veng was on her feet, her left side drenched in splattered mage blood. Her hand clutched her pendant and she exclaimed, 'Item, do thy work.' All the gems in her rings floated up and lazily circled her brow.

Talahan's voice shook. 'I held that spell in my mind so I might cast this.'

Veng took a step back, then another. 'I cannot be harmed by any weapon, or poison, or by any spell in any grimoire, parchment, or scroll written by woman, man, creature, or child.'

'This spell is known to none but me,' Talahan said. 'And it only exists written on the sleeve of my shirt.' He spoke his spell and Veng disappeared.

Veng's army still came at them, but now it was like a snake without a head, writhing blindly. And Queen Zaphron had her own army, barely trained and untried as it was. The defenders of Hardknot Keep formed a dependable core. And then there was Talahan's wall, reinforced and repaired each night by the masons, while Quiet Arthur and the other smiths laboured all day at the forge and anvils.

The Wolfheads left first, three of them coming to the wall to ask permission to take away their dead in their odd yapping voices.

Zaphron immediately agreed. 'What will you do now?'

The three Wolfheads looked at each other.

'Made us this way, Veng did. Bound us to her will.'

'Free we might be, but hated everywhere.'

'Somewhere a new home awaits. Find it, we shall.'

That night a great pyre burned where Veng's army camped and the last of the Wolfheads howled and cried. In the morning they took their spears and loped away.

Attacks on the wall petered out as Veng's army disintegrated. And then one morning the far valley was empty and the army was gone, leaving the wreckage of a passing army among hundreds of smouldering campfires.

It was the tradition in Zangomar to bury the dead. Zaphron asked Little Evelyn if she would like that for Quicksilver.

'I believe Quicksilver decided that this was where he would defy his curse, come what may. It was his choice, so I think yes, he would want that,' Evelyn said. 'He always did like the mountains.'

When she had come to wash and wrap his body, Little Evelyn discovered that the Mer metal had retreated from his body down to the original wound. Now it lay separate from the rest of him, a flawless articulated bronze boot in the shape of a foot.

'I think this needs to be returned to the Mer,' Evelyn said.

Irion agreed. 'We now have two duties to perform.'

Zaphron wanted them to stay, even if it was just for a few weeks. And they tried, they really did, but after two nights in the castle at Steynhylda, despite the comfort of feather beds and baths and clean clothes and good warm fires, that old restlessness grew. And Bobbins, now he was part of Irion's Blades, was ready to see some of the world.

And duty called them: Dante Blackhart and Quicksilver.

Up at the keep the masons began clearing out the rubble from the outer wall gate then decided to tear the whole thing down and rebuild it, gatehouse, walls, and towers, twice as high and deep. The Quicksilver Wall, they called it, and like 'Black Talahan' the name stuck.

That final night Zaphron asked for a feast for everyone who had fought at Hardknot. Brian and Bobbins cooked it, and it was a meal of legend, with flavours, textures, and aromas seldom experienced before. 'Special starter,' Brian said as they served the tables. 'Special main.'

At the end of it, Quiet Arthur diffidently approached Bobbins and placed a cloth roll on the table. Bobbins unwrapped it and revealed three knives, one long, one short, and one heavy. Each had a rosewood handle, the steel patterned like ripples on water from the fold upon fold the smith had made on the steel in the making.

'Thought these might do,' Arthur said.

Bobbins looked at them without touching. 'Yes, they will do very nicely. Thank you, Arthur.'

'Lovely work.' Brian reached in and touched them, one by one, and it was surely a trick of the flickering candlelight that the steel twinkled and glimmered for a moment. 'Beautiful.'

There was no point taking horses, so early next morning Irion, Mace, Little Evelyn, Brian, and Bobbins slipped through the sally port set in the main gate, intending to be well up the high pass by the end of the day.

Talahan and Zaphron waited outside. So did half the population of Steynhylda.

'I do hope you weren't trying to sneak off with the palace silver,' Zaphron said.

Little Evelyn grinned and scratched her head. 'Well, we would have, but Banacort got there first.'

One by one they embraced Zaphron and Talahan. Talahan gave each of them a pleasantly weighty purse. 'Captain's pay, a year in advance. Just in case you change your minds.'

The tradition on Zangomar is not to kneel, or cheer, but to clap hands. Queen Zaphron began, followed by Talahan, and then the gathered throng. Irion's Blades walked through the applause, past their smiles and children holding out possies of wild flowers. All down the Market Way they walked, and out through the town gates.

By noon they were high above Steynhylda, where a young goatherd watched them go with eyes as round as saucers.

By nightfall they were still some miles from the highest reaches of the pass. Already the air was thin, cold, and dry. Irion shivered by the fire, wrapped in her furs.

Bobbins looked down into the broad valley that was the kingdom of Zangomar. The entirety of his life so far lay there.

In the distance the warm lights of Steynhylda glimmered. Even further away a single light shone and he wondered if Quiet Arthur sat drinking in the First and Last.

Mace stood beside him. 'It's strange to think Veng is still out there, in that sideways place Talahan's spell put her.'

'She got what she wanted, to rule a world at peace. I hope she enjoys it.'

'Hmm.'

The next day they came across the first of a scattered line of a dozen horses expired from the cold dry air. Further on they discovered Bon Banacort as he worked with half-frozen fingers unloading silver and gold from saddle packs into a smaller bag which he had been lugging up and over the pass, and back again. His lips were cracked, dark circles rimmed his eyes, his fingernails had started to blacken. Half crouched beside a horse's corpse, he watched them pass without a word.

Little Evelyn was the last to go by. As she did, she paused, snapped her fingers, and turned back. 'Here's one for you:

Trust not those cunning waters of his eyes,
For villainy is not without such rheum;
And he, long traded in it, makes it seem
Like rivers of remorse and innocency.'

Bannacort made no reply and without looking back Little Evelyn walked on.

*

The next morning the young goatherd could be found jumping from rock to tussock, cutting grass heads with his switch as he re-enacted the defence of Hardknot Keep. Some way off a red-tailed hawk hovered, and if it turned its gaze it would have seen a man walking in the deep distance. He made his way towards a small farm in the hills far beyond Steynhylda where his parents still lived. Though very old now, they had seen him coming, and sat holding hands, and watched, and waited.

Author's Note: Little Evelyn's quotation on the last page is taken from King John *by* William Shakespeare. *I take responsibility for Bon Banacourt's atrocious prose.*

About the Author

David Gullen is a two-time winner of the British Fantasy Society Short Story competition. His work has appeared in *The Best of British SF 2020*, and *2021, F&SF, Tales from the Magician's Skull*, and more. Other work has been short-listed for the James White Award and placed in the Aeon Award.

Once Upon a Parsec: the Book of Alien Fairy Tales, for which he was the editor, and his SF novel *Shopocalypse* are both available from NewCon.

Born in Africa and baptised by King Neptune, David has lived in England for most of his life. He currently lives behind several tree ferns in South London with his wife, fantasy writer Gaie Sebold, and the nicest cat you ever did see. Find out more at www.davidgullen.com.

ALSO FROM NEWCON PRESS

Best of British Science Fiction 2022 ed. by Donna Scott
Editor Donna Scott has scoured magazines, anthologies, webzines and obscure genre corners to discover the very best science fiction stories by British and British-based authors published during 2022. A thrilling blend of cutting-edge and traditional, showcasing all that makes science fiction the most entertaining genre around.

The Book of Gaheris – Kari Sperring
Gaheris of Orkney, one aof the less celebrated knights of Arthur's court, finds himself up to his neck in intrigue, deception, violence, murder, and old secrets. Clouds gather over Camelot, threatening to destroy all that Arthur and Guenever have built, and Gaheris may be all that stands between Arthur's noble kingdom and disaster.

Sparks Flying – Kim Lakin
First ever collection from critically acclaimed author Kim Lakin, spanning fourteen years of writing. Her very best short stories, as selected by the author herself. Fourteen expertly crafted tales that span myth, science fiction, industrial grime and darkest imagining.

The Wild Hunt – Garry Kilworth
When Gods meddle in the affairs of mortals, it never ends well… for the mortals, at any rate. Steeped in ancient law, history and imagination, Garry Kilworth serves up an epic Anglo-Saxon saga of swordplay, witches, giants, dwarfs, elves and more, as a young warrior wrongly accused of patricide sets out to clear his name and regain his birthright.

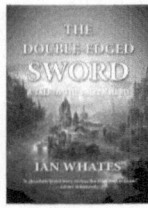

The Double-Edged Sword – Ian Whates
A disgraced swordsman leaves town one step ahead of justice. His past, however, soon catches up with him in the form of Julia, a notorious thief and sometimes assassin. Thrust into an impossible situation, he embarks on what will surely prove to be a suicide mission. "A cheerfully brutal story of betrayal and skulduggery, vicious fun." *– Adrian Tchaikovsky*

www.newconpress.co.uk

www.ingramcontent.com/pod-product-compliance
Lightning Source LLC
Chambersburg PA
CBHW032107170626
46808CB00008B/2977